WHAT THE SEA KEEPS

E. M. Rossi

The Reading Glass Books
1-888-420-3050
www.readingglassbooks.com
production@readingglassbooks.com

Table of Contents

CHAPTER

One

The Brass Plaque

The lighthouse had stood on Blackthorn Point for one hundred and forty-seven years, according to the brass plaque half-hidden by lichen beside the door. Elias Callahan ran his thumb across the raised letters as if he could read the age of the metal itself. The plaque was cool, damp, and slightly pitted, the way everything here seemed to be—touched by the sea even when the sea was half a mile away at low tide.

Mara stood a step behind him, yellow rain boots bright against the gray stone path, arms folded across the front of her faded denim jacket. "One hundred and forty-seven," she echoed, tasting the number. "That's older than both our grandmothers combined. Think it's haunted yet?"

Elias laughed, the sound short and easy, the way it always was when she teased him. "Only if the ghost pays half the mortgage."

1

They had driven four hours from the city that morning, the U-Haul rattling behind their old Subaru like a reluctant chaperone. The city had been all concrete and sirens and the constant low hum of too many people breathing the same recycled air. They had wanted quiet. They had wanted distance. They had wanted a place where the sky was bigger than their worries. Blackthorn Point had seemed to answer every question on the realtor's listing: historic residence, panoramic views, private shoreline access. The price was suspiciously low for a structure that size, but the realtor had shrugged and said the last owner had moved to Florida for his arthritis. No one had lived here full-time since 1978.

They didn't ask why.

The key was heavy in Elias's palm—an actual iron skeleton key, the kind you see in movies. It turned with a gritty complaint, and the front door swung inward on hinges that needed oil. Inside, the air smelled of salt, old wood, and something faintly metallic, like pennies left in rain. The main floor was one open room: kitchen on the left with a cast-iron stove that looked older than the plaque outside, living area on the right with built-in bookshelves warped by decades of moisture. A spiral iron staircase rose through the center like a spine, climbing into the tower.

Mara dropped her duffel bag on the scarred pine floor and spun slowly, arms out. "It's perfect," she said, and for once she wasn't exaggerating. Sunlight slanted through the tall, salt-frosted windows and painted rectangles of gold across the planks. Dust motes danced like tiny planets. She crossed to the nearest window and pressed her forehead to the glass. "Look at that water. You can see the curve of the earth from here."

Elias set the grocery bags on the counter and joined her. Below them the Atlantic stretched out, restless and slate-colored even on a clear day. A small aluminum skiff bobbed at the private dock, chained to a cleat. The tide was coming in; the waves already licked at the rocks with white tongues. He slipped an arm around her waist and felt the familiar warmth of her body against his. Chestnut hair tickled his chin. She smelled like the coffee they'd stopped for three hours ago and the vanilla lotion she'd used that morning.

"We're really doing this," he said quietly.

"We're really doing this."

They spent the rest of the afternoon unloading. The U-Haul contained everything they had decided mattered: her fishing rods and tackle boxes, his cast-iron pans and knife roll, a battered leather couch, a queen mattress still in its plastic, two boxes of books, one box of records, and the fairy lights she had insisted on bringing even though the tower had no outlets above the second landing. Elias carried the mattress up the spiral stairs twice—once to the bedroom they claimed on the second floor, once back down because Mara decided she wanted the bed under the lantern room itself so they could fall asleep under the stars. By the time the sun dropped behind the western headland they were both sweaty, laughing, and covered in dust.

That first night they ate cold pizza on the floor because the stove hadn't been lit yet. The wind had picked up, and the old iron weathervane on the roof—shaped like a leaping marlin—screamed every time it swung north. Mara lay with her head in Elias's lap, pointing out constellations through the lantern-room glass.

"You hear that?" she asked after a while.

"The wind?"

"No. Under the wind. Like… footsteps. Up in the tower."

He listened. There was only the sea and the weathervane and the soft creak of the house settling. "Old buildings talk," he said. "Especially ones that have watched the ocean for a century and a half. It's probably just the tide moving the rocks."

She smiled, unconvinced but willing to let it go. "Promise you'll protect me from the ghost fishwives?"

"On my honor as a future lighthouse keeper."

They fell asleep tangled together under a single sleeping bag, the fairy lights twinkling along the iron railing like captured stars.

The next nine days blurred into a gentle rhythm that felt almost stolen. Elias woke first each morning, brewed coffee on the ancient stove after he figured out how to coax it to life, and stood at the kitchen window watching the tide. Mara would pad down later in one of his flannel shirts, hair loose and sleep-mussed, and kiss the back of his neck while he scrambled eggs. They explored every inch of the property. The cellar was a maze of stone arches and old lobster traps; the tower stairs were narrow and treacherous, but the view from the lantern room made every creak worth it. On clear days they could see three other lighthouses along the coast, tiny white dots against the horizon like distant cousins waving.

Mara claimed the skiff immediately. She had grown up on a lake in Vermont, but the ocean was new and intoxicating. She spent hours on the dock restringing lines, sharpening hooks, studying tide charts she'd printed from the library in town. "The mackerel run is supposed to be early this year," she told him on the fourth morning, dangling a silver lure that flashed in the sun. "I'm going to catch our dinner every night until you beg for mercy."

Elias, who had trained as a sous-chef in the city and still dreamed in sauces and reductions, only grinned. "Bring me something worth filleting and I'll make you a feast you'll never forget."

They kept their promises. She brought back bluefish and striped bass; he turned them into pan-seared fillets with brown-butter sage or simple ceviche when the day was too warm. They ate on the rocks at sunset, wine in coffee mugs because they hadn't unpacked the good glasses yet. At night they made love in the lantern room, the iron bed creaking in time with the waves, the fairy lights casting soft shadows across their skin. The isolation wrapped around them like a blanket. No emails. No deadlines. No neighbors. Just the two of them and the sea.

But the house noticed.

Small things, at first. The weathervane screamed louder on certain nights, always when Mara was asleep and Elias was reading by the stove. Once he found the cellar door unlatched though he was certain he'd bolted it. Another morning the brass plaque outside had been wiped clean of lichen, as if someone had polished it in the dark. He told himself it was the salt air, the wind, his own distraction. Mara never mentioned the footsteps again, but sometimes he caught her glancing up the spiral stairs when she thought he wasn't looking.

On the ninth evening they sat on the dock with their feet in the cold water. The sky was the color of wet slate, and a light mist had begun to fall—nothing serious, just the kind of rain that feels like the ocean exhaling.

"I'm going out tomorrow," Mara said suddenly.

Elias looked sideways at her. "Forecast says it might pick up."

"It's light rain. Fish get lazy in this stuff. They'll be right under the surface, easy pickings." She leaned against his shoulder. "I'll be back before you even start chopping onions. Promise."

He smiled because her excitement was contagious. "Don't let the mermaids steal you."

She kissed the top of his head, the way she always did when she was feeling tender. "They'd have to catch me first."

They walked back up the stone steps together, boots crunching on wet gravel. Inside, Elias lit the stove and began laying out ingredients for the stew he'd been planning—carrots, celery, a bottle of red he'd been saving. Mara hummed while she sorted her tackle box on the kitchen table. The rain tapped the metal roof like polite fingernails. Neither of them felt the slightest worry.

Outside, the weathervane turned once, slowly, as if tasting the change in the wind.

And the lighthouse, one hundred and forty-seven years old, kept its secrets the way it always had: patiently, quietly, and forever.

Two

The Keeper's Log

The rain held off longer than the forecast promised.

For ten more days after that first misty evening on the dock, the weather stayed gentle—cool mornings, afternoons bright enough to make the Atlantic look almost friendly, evenings that cooled slowly into star-scattered dark. Mara and Elias sank deeper into the rhythm of the lighthouse as though the house itself had decided to let them breathe.

They unpacked the last boxes on the morning of the twelfth day. Elias carried the record player up to the lantern room because Mara said she wanted to hear jazz while the stars came out. She strung the fairy lights in looping garlands along the iron railing, then again along the curved wall, until the whole space glowed soft amber at night. They pushed the iron bed against the windows so they could wake to the horizon instead of a wall. The first night they slept there, Mara traced constellations on his bare back with one fingertip and whispered names she half-remembered from childhood books: Cassiopeia, Orion, the faint smear of the Milky Way that city lights had stolen from them years ago.

"You know this place is older than the country it's in," she said one afternoon while they sat on the rocks below the tower, sharing a thermos of coffee. The tide was out; the exposed seaweed smelled sharp and green.

"Older than the Constitution," Elias agreed. "The plaque says 1878. That's pre-electricity, pre-telephone. They lit this thing with whale oil."

Mara tilted her head back to look up the white tower. "Imagine being the keeper back then. Alone. Waiting for ships that might never come. Just you and the lamp and the dark."

Elias watched her profile—the way the wind lifted strands of chestnut hair across her cheek—and felt a quiet ache of gratitude. "We're not alone," he said.

She turned and kissed him, tasting of coffee and salt. "No. We're definitely not."

They explored the property in widening circles. The path behind the lighthouse wound through scrub pine and wild blackberry canes to a small shingle beach no bigger than a parking lot. Mara collected beach glass there—pale green, sea-smoothed amber, one rare piece of deep cobalt she kept in her pocket like a talisman. Elias found an old iron ring bolt cemented into the rock, half-buried in barnacles; he scraped it clean with his thumbnail and wondered who had last tied a boat there, and why they had never come back for it.

Inside, the house revealed itself slowly, the way old buildings do when they're not in a hurry to be known. The kitchen drawers stuck unless you lifted them just so. The floorboards in the living room creaked a particular three-note pattern when you crossed near the bookshelf. One evening Mara discovered a narrow cupboard behind the pantry door—barely wide enough for a person—containing three dusty bottles of homemade elderberry wine and a single brass key with no obvious lock to fit it. She hung the key on a nail above the stove "for luck," she said.

They cooked together most nights. Elias taught her how to make a proper beurre blanc; she showed him how to clean a fish without wasting a scrap. They ate at the scarred pine table with the windows open, listening to the waves and the occasional cry of a gull. Sometimes they talked about the future—maybe a garden in the sheltered lee of the tower, maybe solar panels on the south slope, maybe a dog someday when the money stretched further. Sometimes they didn't talk at all, just sat with their feet touching under the table, content in the silence.

On the fifteenth day Mara found the first keeper's log.

She had gone down to the cellar to look for more wine glasses. Elias heard her call up the stairs, voice muffled by stone.

"Eli! Come look at this."

He descended into the cool dark. She stood beside the tall wooden cabinet, one ledger already in her hands. Dust drifted in the beam of her phone flashlight.

"Blackthorn Light – Keeper's Log," she read aloud. "1879 to 1884. There's a whole row of them."

They carried four volumes upstairs to the kitchen table. Elias poured them each a glass of the elderberry wine—thick, sweet, faintly medicinal—and they opened the first book side by side.

Captain Josiah Hale's handwriting was careful, almost elegant. Entries began with weather, oil levels, vessels sighted. Then came the personal notes.

3 November 1880 – Abigail complains of drafts in the lantern room though all windows are latched. Says she hears skirts brushing the iron stairs at night. Told her it is only the house settling after a century of gales.

Mara's finger paused on the page. "Abigail. The wife."

They turned pages slowly. The entries grew shorter, terser.

19 January 1881 – Abigail will not climb above the second landing after dark. Claims a woman with long pale hair stands at the south window, watching the sea. Hair not hers. Advised rest and warm broth.

Elias felt the hairs on his forearms lift. Mara reached for his hand without looking away from the page.

The last entry mentioning Abigail was brief:

22 January 1881 – Wife took the dinghy at midday despite light snow. Boat returned at first light, secured properly. No sign of her. Search parties dispatched. May God have mercy.

Silence settled over the kitchen. Outside, the wind had picked up a little, rattling a loose pane in the living room. Mara closed the ledger gently.

"That's… eerie," she said.

"Yeah."

They looked at each other. Neither laughed it off. Neither rushed to open the next volume.

Instead Mara stood, crossed to the stove, and put the kettle on. "Tea?" she asked, as though they needed something ordinary to anchor them.

Elias nodded. While the water heated, he flipped to the back of the ledger, where a later keeper had taped in a yellowed newspaper clipping from 1923. The headline read: LOCAL WOMAN LOST AT SEA IN SUDDEN SQUALL.

The photograph showed a young woman with long, light hair, staring straight into the camera with eyes that looked almost silver in the grainy print. Lillian Voss, wife of Keeper Thomas Voss.

Mara read the caption aloud. "Disappeared while checking lobster pots. Vessel recovered undamaged. Search suspended after three days."

They sat with that for a while. The kettle whistled. Mara poured chamomile into two mugs and carried them back to the table.

"Do you think it's just bad luck?" she asked quietly. "Women and the sea here?"

"Or bad weather," Elias said. "Storms come up fast on this coast. Always have."

She nodded, but her eyes kept drifting to the south window—the one that looked straight out over the water toward the point where the skiff was tied. "Still. It's strange. Three different keepers, three wives, same pattern."

"Two," Elias corrected. "We only have two stories so far."

Mara gave a small, crooked smile. "Let's not open the next book tonight."

They didn't.

That night they made love in the lantern room with the fairy lights on low. Afterward Mara curled against his chest, listening to his heartbeat slow. "Promise me something," she murmured.

"Anything."

"If I ever go out in the boat and don't come back right away… don't wait too long to call for help."

He kissed the top of her head. "I won't have to. You always come back."

She laughed softly. "True. I'm too stubborn to drown."

They fell asleep to the sound of the waves and the faint, rhythmic creak of the tower settling into itself.

The next morning dawned clear. Mara went down to the dock to check the skiff's lines and bail out the overnight rainwater. Elias watched from the kitchen window while he chopped vegetables for lunch. She waved up at him, yellow slicker bright against the gray rocks. He waved back.

The lighthouse stood quiet around them.

CHAPTER

Three

Salt and Sound

The lighthouse smelled different depending on the hour.

At dawn it carried the clean, mineral bite of night-cooled stone and the faint metallic tang of the brass fittings Elias had begun polishing on idle mornings. By mid-morning the kitchen overtook everything: coffee grounds steeping dark and bitter in the old percolator, the buttery warmth of toast browning under the broiler, the sharp citrus snap of Mara squeezing lemons over fresh-caught mackerel fillets they'd eaten the night before. Afternoon brought the sea indoors on the wind—brine so thick you could taste it on your tongue, mixed with the sweet rot of drying kelp that clung to the rocks below and the green, almost grassy scent of the wild thyme Mara had transplanted into clay pots along the south wall.

Evenings were quieter in smell but louder in sound. The iron weathervane on the roof turned with a high, keening scrape when the breeze shifted north, like fingernails dragged slowly across slate. The waves didn't crash so much as sigh against the point, a low, wet exhalation that rolled up through the floorboards and into the soles of their feet. Inside, the house answered in small, private ways: the soft pop of the woodstove settling as coals cooled, the tick of the grandfather clock in the living room (which they'd found stopped at 3:17 and never bothered to wind), the occasional groan of the spiral staircase as it cooled after a day of sun.

Mara loved the sounds most.

She said so one evening in their third week, lying on the rug in front of the stove with her head in Elias's lap. He was reading one of the keeper's logs by lamplight—carefully now, after the first unsettling entries—while she traced idle patterns on his knee with her fingertip.

"Listen," she whispered.

He lowered the book. The wind was light, barely enough to stir the curtains, but it found the loose pane in the south window and made it rattle in soft, irregular Morse code. Beyond that, the sea murmured steadily, a thousand small pebbles shifting under each retreating wave.

"It's like the house is breathing with the tide," she said. "In… out… in… out."

Elias set the log aside and ran his fingers through her hair—chestnut strands still sun-warmed from the afternoon she'd spent on the dock mending nets. "You're getting poetic on me."

"I'm getting observant." She rolled onto her back so she could look up at him. Her hazel eyes caught the firelight, flecked with gold. "You hear it too. Don't pretend."

He did. He'd noticed how the sounds changed when Mara was near the water. The gulls seemed louder when she laughed on the rocks; the waves seemed to hush when she stood at the dock's edge, rod in hand, waiting for a bite. It was as though the place recognized her rhythm and matched it.

They spent the next days mapping the lighthouse the way lovers map each other—slowly, deliberately, without hurry.

Mara discovered that the cellar stairs creaked in a descending scale, each step a half-note lower until you reached the stone floor, where the echo swallowed sound entirely. She tested it barefoot one morning, laughing as the notes dropped away beneath her. Elias followed her down with a flashlight, pretending to be annoyed, but he stayed close enough that their shadows merged on the damp walls.

Upstairs, in the lantern room, the fairy lights they'd strung cast trembling reflections across the curved glass. At night the patterns danced on the ceiling like schools of silver fish. Mara would lie on her back and watch them while Elias read aloud from old shipping logs he'd found tucked behind the bookshelves—dry accounts of wrecks and rescues that somehow felt intimate in the warm glow.

One afternoon she climbed the exterior ladder to the catwalk—against Elias's half-hearted protests—and stood with her arms out, letting the wind push against her palms. When she came down her cheeks were flushed, hair wild, eyes bright.

"It's like standing inside the storm before it arrives," she said, breathless. "You can feel it gathering out there. Waiting."

Elias pulled her inside and kissed the salt from her lips. "Stay inside the next time it gathers."

She only grinned. "Where's the fun in that?"

They began small rituals. Every third morning Mara brewed coffee and carried two mugs up to the lantern room so they could watch the sun rise over the water—first a thin pink line, then a slow bleed of orange, then full gold that turned the waves to molten metal. Elias would wrap his arms around her from behind, chin on her shoulder, and they'd stand in silence until the light became too bright to look at directly.

In the evenings he cooked while she cleaned fish at the outdoor sink he'd rigged beside the door. The knife made wet, rhythmic snicks against the cutting board; water hissed from the spigot; scales glittered on the stone like scattered coins. She hummed old sea shanties she'd learned from her grandfather—low, rolling tunes about lost ships and faithless lovers—and Elias found himself matching the tempo with his chopping knife.

The house seemed to approve. The weathervane turned smoothly now, almost musically. Doors that had stuck loosened. The brass plaque outside the front door gleamed brighter each week, though neither of them had touched it since the day they arrived.

They read more of the logs together, treating them like ghost stories told around a campfire rather than warnings.

Thomas Voss's entries from the 1920s were the most vivid. He wrote of Lillian in careful, restrained prose, as though afraid too much emotion would stain the page.

14 June 1923 – Lillian insists the south window is colder than the rest. She stands there for hours, hair loose, watching nothing. I asked what she sees. She said, "What the sea keeps."

Mara shivered when she read that line aloud. "What the sea keeps," she repeated softly. "That's beautiful. And awful."

Elias closed the book. "Let's leave the rest for another night."

They did. Instead they opened the elderberry wine again—thicker now, almost syrupy—and danced slowly in the lantern room to a scratchy record of Billie Holiday. Mara's bare feet were cool against the iron floor; Elias's hands warm at the small of her back. When the song ended they stayed swaying a moment longer, the needle ticking in the silence.

"I love this place," Mara said against his chest. "Even the sad parts. It feels… honest."

Elias kissed her forehead. "It's ours now. Sad parts and all."

Outside, the tide turned. The waves grew a little louder, a little closer. A single gull cried once, sharp and lonely, then was gone.

The next morning Mara woke early. She slipped out of bed without waking Elias, padded down the spiral stairs in one of his old T-shirts, and stood at the kitchen window watching the water. The sky was the color of wet slate again—same as that first misty day—but the air felt heavier, expectant.

She made coffee, carried a mug back upstairs, and sat on the edge of the bed until Elias stirred.

"Light rain coming," she said when his eyes opened. "Perfect fishing weather."

He smiled sleepily. "You're going out?"

"Just for a couple hours. Fish are lazy in this stuff. I'll be back before you start the stew."

He reached for her hand, tugged her down beside him. "Promise?"

She kissed him slow and lingering, tasting of coffee and morning. "Promise."

They lingered in bed a while longer, listening to the first soft taps of rain on the metal roof—like fingernails, polite at first, asking permission to enter.

Neither of them felt the slightest worry.

The lighthouse held its breath around them, salt-scented and quiet, content—for now—to let them believe the past was only stories written in old ink.

CHAPTER

Four

The Light Rain

The rain began while Mara was still loading the skiff.

From the lantern-room window Elias watched the first drops darken the stones of the path in small, scattered coins. They fell slowly at first, almost hesitant, as though the sky were trying them out. Mara didn't even glance up; she was already kneeling on the dock planks, double-checking the bow line, her yellow slicker gleaming wet under the low gray light. The outboard motor cover was off, fuel line connected, the small red tank sloshing faintly as she gave it a shake.

Elias leaned his forehead against the cold curved glass. The fairy lights still glowed along the railing behind him—soft amber beads that made the iron bed and rumpled sheets look warmer than they were. He could still taste the coffee on his tongue, still feel the press of her lips from the goodbye kiss she'd given him ten minutes earlier, slow and unhurried, her hands cupping his face for a long second before she pulled away with that crooked smile.

"Back before the onions even sweat," she'd promised.

He had believed her.

Now he watched her swing one leg over the gunwale, settle onto the thwart, and pull the starter cord. The motor coughed once, twice, then caught with a low, steady burble that carried up the rocks even through the thickening rain. She gave the throttle a gentle twist; the skiff eased away from the cleat, carving a clean, widening V through the flat water. At the mouth of the little cove she turned starboard, rounding the black rocks of the point without looking back.

The boat disappeared behind the headland.

Elias stayed at the window a moment longer, watching the empty water where she had been. The rain strengthened—still light, still polite, tapping the metal roof in a rhythm that almost matched his pulse. He turned away, descended the spiral stairs (each step giving its familiar descending creak), and stepped into the kitchen.

The house smelled of morning: coffee grounds cooling in the percolator, the faint vanilla that clung to everything Mara touched, the clean linen scent of the dish towel still folded on the counter from breakfast. He lit the stove, set the Dutch oven over the flame, dropped in a generous knob of butter. It hissed and foamed immediately, the rich yellow melting into a golden pool. He added the onions he'd already sliced—half-moons translucent at the edges—and stirred them slowly with a wooden spoon. The sharp sweetness rose in warm waves, fogging the nearest window.

Carrots next. He diced them into bright batons that snapped under the knife, the sound crisp against the growing patter outside. Celery followed, strings peeling away in long pale threads that he swept aside. The ginger came last—grated fine on the microplane, its citrus-sharp perfume cutting through the butter and onion like a clean blade. A bay leaf, a sprig of rosemary from the clay pot on the sill (Mara had started it from a cutting she'd found growing wild behind the tower), salt, a few cracks of black pepper.

He seared the chuck roast in the same pot, the meat sizzling dark at the edges, fat rendering into shimmering liquid. The aroma deepened—savory, rich, almost meaty comfort. He poured in the Bordeaux, watching the deep red wine hiss and steam as it met the heat, the alcohol burning off in fragrant clouds that carried notes of black cherry and damp earth. He scraped the browned bits from the bottom with the spoon, stirred everything together, set the lid ajar, and turned the flame low.

The stew began its slow simmer.

He poured the rest of the wine into a coffee mug—because the good glasses were still in a box somewhere upstairs—and carried it to the south window. The rain was heavier now, individual drops striking the glass with soft thuds before sliding down in long, trembling trails. The water beyond had lost its earlier calm; small whitecaps flecked the surface, racing in uneven ranks toward the rocks. The wind had found its voice—a low moan under the rain that rose and fell like breathing.

He checked the clock on the wall: 4:18. She'd been gone barely an hour. Plenty of time.

He sipped the wine. It was warm on his tongue, smooth, grounding.

Outside, the weathervane gave its first slow scrape, metal on metal, testing the new direction of the gusts. The loose pane in the living room rattled once, then again. Elias crossed to it, pressed his palm against the wood to still the vibration. The house answered with a soft creak somewhere in the walls, as though shifting its weight.

He returned to the stove, lifted the lid, stirred. The stew bubbled gently, carrots softening, meat beginning to yield. The kitchen was warm now, the windows fogged completely, the world outside reduced to gray streaks and muffled sound.

He tried not to look at the clock again.

By 5:40 the wind was no longer moaning; it was growling. The rain lashed the roof in sheets, the metal ringing like a struck bell. The weathervane shrieked—a high, metallic wail that rose with every gust and cut off abruptly when the wind shifted. Elias stood at the kitchen door, slicker on, hood up, staring down at the dock.

The chain was still coiled where she'd left it. No skiff. No running light. Only the black water churning against the pilings, spray lifting in white bursts that stung his face even from thirty feet above.

He called her name into the storm. Once. Twice. The sound shredded instantly.

Back inside he grabbed the VHF from the shelf, thumbed channel 16.

Static hissed. Then nothing.

He tried her cell. Straight to voicemail. Her voice—bright, laughing—filled the kitchen for three seconds: Hey, it's Mara. I'm probably catching dinner. Leave a message.

He left one. Then another. Then a third, shorter, quieter.

"Mara. Come home."

He called the coast guard at 7:14 p.m.

The dispatcher's voice was calm, professional, kind in the way people are when they've said these words before. She asked for details he gave in short bursts: aluminum skiff, fourteen feet, green hull, yellow slicker, chestnut hair, hazel eyes, left at approximately 3:15, promised to be back by five. He spelled her name twice because his throat had closed.

"They're launching the cutter," she said. "Local boats are already putting out. Stay by the radio."

He did not stay by the radio.

He climbed to the lantern room, stood at the south window, fairy lights still glowing behind him like a constellation he no longer trusted. Searchlights appeared after nine—thin white beams slicing the dark, sweeping slow arcs across the black water. Red and green running lights bobbed closer: village boats, men in oilskins who knew these waters better than anyone. Voices crackled over the VHF in terse fragments.

Nothing.

The wind screamed highest around midnight. Rain hammered the glass so hard he thought it might crack. The tower itself seemed to sway—subtle, almost imperceptible, but enough to make the fairy lights swing on their strings.

Elias did not sleep.

Dawn came thin and gray, reluctant to show itself. The rain had eased to a steady drizzle, almost mocking in its gentleness. The cutter tied up at the dock long enough for Captain Ruiz to climb the stone steps, boots heavy, oilskin dripping.

"We'll go again when the light's better," he said, voice low. "You should try to rest."

Elias nodded because words were too heavy.

He went back to the kitchen. The stew had gone cold, surface skimmed with pale fat. He scraped it into a container without looking at it, started fresh coffee because his hands shook when they were empty.

The keeper's log lay open on the table—Mara's bookmark still in place at Thomas Voss's entry.

17 July 1923 – Lillian took the skiff at 3 p.m. Light rain. Promised to return for supper. Storm rose without warning. Boat found at dawn, bow line doubled, knot perfect. She is gone.

Elias stared at the page until the letters blurred.

He lifted his eyes to the south window.

For one heartbeat the silhouette was there—long pale hair catching the weak morning light, head turned toward the sea, then gone as though it had never been.

Not chestnut.

Not hazel.

He exhaled slowly.

The rain kept falling.

The lighthouse waited.

Five

The Long Gray

The silhouette vanished so quickly Elias wasn't certain it had been there at all.

He blinked hard, once, twice, the weak dawn light stinging his eyes. The south window showed only rain-streaked glass and the blurred line where sea met sky. No pale hair. No turned head. Just the same empty view that had mocked him all night.

He exhaled through his teeth, the sound ragged in the quiet kitchen. The coffee he'd started was ready; he poured a mug without measuring, black and scalding, and carried it to the table. The keeper's log stayed closed beside his elbow like an accusation he wasn't ready to answer yet.

Outside, the drizzle continued—soft, steady, almost companionable now that the worst of the wind had spent itself. The cutter had pulled away again at first light, engines throbbing low as it nosed back into the swells. Captain Ruiz had left a card on the kitchen counter before he went: Coast Guard contact numbers, a local marine salvage number, the name of a grief counselor in the next town over. Elias hadn't touched any of it.

He drank the coffee standing up. It tasted like ash and copper.

The search resumed at 0700. He heard the boats before he saw them—diesel rumble carrying over the water, voices shouting coordinates, the occasional metallic clang of gear being shifted. He climbed to the lantern room again, stood at the railing of the catwalk despite the slick iron and the lingering spray. Below, three village boats fanned out in a loose line: the Mary Rose, a battered lobster boat with red hull; the Sea Sparrow, smaller, faster, painted white; and an open skiff manned by two men in matching yellow oilskins who looked barely old enough to shave. They moved methodically, quartering the water between Blackthorn Point and the outer ledges where the bottom dropped away to sixty feet.

Elias watched until his fingers went numb on the railing. No one waved up at him. No one shouted good news.

By noon the drizzle had thickened to a soaking mist that clung to everything. He came down to the kitchen, made more coffee, forced himself to eat a slice of the bread Mara had baked two days earlier—still soft in the middle, crust dark and crisp. He chewed without tasting, swallowed without pleasure. The stew container sat in the fridge; he couldn't bring himself to open it.

The VHF crackled sporadically. Fragments of conversation drifted through:

"…negative on the third sector…"

"…current's running strong today, anything could've drifted…"

"…keep the pattern tight, boys…"

He answered every check-in from the cutter. His voice sounded foreign to him—flat, mechanical, a recording of someone else's grief.

Afternoon blurred into evening. The boats came and went in shifts. Local fishermen brought thermoses of soup and foil-wrapped sandwiches to the dock; Elias accepted them with nods he hoped looked grateful. He left the food untouched on the counter until it cooled, then wrapped it again and set it aside for tomorrow.

Night fell early, the gray bleeding into black without any real transition. The searchlights returned—brighter now, cutting sharper paths across the water. Elias stood at the south window again, fairy lights still on behind him because the dark felt too absolute without them. He counted the beams: five tonight, maybe six. More volunteers had come from farther down the coast.

He spoke to the empty room once, quietly.

"Come back, Mara."

The house answered with a soft creak from the spiral stairs, nothing more.

The second day was worse.

The mist lifted around ten, revealing a sea still restless but no longer furious. The cutter ran parallel search grids; the village boats worked closer to shore, checking every cove and rock pile. A state police helicopter joined them at noon—low passes, rotor wash flattening the wave tops, the downdraft loud enough to rattle the loose pane again. Elias stood outside on the landing, neck craned, watching the machine bank and turn. No signal flare. No debris spotted. Just the steady thump-thump-thump fading westward.

He walked the shoreline himself in the afternoon, boots sinking into wet shingle, eyes scanning every piece of driftwood, every clump of weed. He found a single blue fishing lure tangled in kelp—identical to the ones Mara kept in her tackle box—but no line attached, no hook bent, no sign it had been torn free in struggle. He pocketed it anyway, fingers closing tight around the cold metal.

That night he slept for the first time—fifteen minutes on the couch, fully clothed, waking with a start when the weathervane scraped in a sudden gust. He thought he'd heard her voice calling from the lantern room. He climbed the stairs two at a time, heart hammering.

Empty.

The third day brought rain again—proper rain, steady and cold. The search slowed; visibility dropped to a quarter mile. The helicopter stayed grounded. The boats ran tighter patterns, closer to the point. Elias stood at the dock for hours, slicker hood dripping into his eyes, watching them circle the same water they'd already searched twice.

A fisherman named Cal—gray beard, hands like knotted rope—tied up around dusk and climbed the steps to speak to him.

"We're not giving up," Cal said, voice rough from shouting over engines. "But the tide's been running hard. If she went in…"

He didn't finish. He didn't need to.

Elias nodded. "Thank you."

Cal looked at him a long moment. "You eaten anything today?"

Elias shook his head.

Cal pressed a paper bag into his hands—still-warm biscuits, a container of chowder thick with clams. "Eat. She'd want you to."

Elias carried the food inside. He set it on the counter, opened the lid. The steam rose, carrying the scent of salt pork and thyme. He stared at it until it cooled, then covered it again.

The fourth day the wind shifted west, bringing clearer skies but colder air. The search expanded—boats working the outer banks, the helicopter back in the air. Elias drove into town for the first time since the disappearance, hands tight on the wheel, eyes flicking to the water every time the road curved close to the shore.

The library was quiet. Mrs. Hargrove recognized him immediately.

"I heard," she said softly. "I'm so sorry."

He asked for anything more on the lighthouse. Anything on the keepers' wives. Anything that might explain why the same story kept repeating.

She hesitated, then pulled a thin file from behind the desk—yellowed clippings, photocopied pages from old town records. She slid it across without a word.

He read sitting at a small table by the window. Abigail Hale, 1881. Lillian Voss, 1923. A third name he hadn't seen before—Eleanor Price, 1957. Each entry ended the same way: light rain, skiff, storm, boat returned empty.

No bodies ever found.

He copied the names into a notebook with shaking hands. When he looked up, Mrs. Hargrove was watching him.

"Some places hold on to things," she said quietly. "Or people."

He drove back in silence, notebook on the passenger seat like a weight.

That night he stood at the south window again.

The silhouette returned.

Long pale hair, almost luminous in the moonlight that had broken through the clouds. The figure didn't move at first—just stood, facing the sea. Then slowly, deliberately, it turned.

Not Mara's face.

Eyes too wide, too bright. Hair the color of winter surf.

Elias stepped closer to the glass. His breath fogged it.

"Who are you?" he whispered.

The figure tilted its head—as though listening—then dissolved into shadow.

He stayed there until dawn, whispering questions to the empty window.

The search continued.

The lighthouse listened.

CHAPTER

Six

The Boat Returns

The sixth day broke cold and clear, the kind of brittle morning that makes every sound sharper: the crunch of gravel under boots, the distant clang of a bell buoy rolling in the swell, the low mutter of engines as the search boats idled back out from the harbor.

Elias stood on the landing before the sun had fully cleared the horizon, coffee gone cold in his hand, eyes fixed on the water. The mist had burned off early; the Atlantic lay flat and gunmetal under a sky the color of new tin. He could see farther today than he had since the storm—every rock, every breaking wavelet, every empty stretch where a yellow slicker should have been.

No one had called off the search. Not officially. But the pattern had changed. Fewer boats now. Wider grids. Voices on the VHF quieter, more resigned. Captain Ruiz had stopped climbing

36

the steps himself; he radioed updates twice a day instead. Elias answered each time with the same three words: "Still nothing."

He walked the shoreline again after breakfast—nothing more than dry toast he forced down because his stomach had started cramping when it was empty too long. The shingle crunched under his boots; wet kelp popped and tore. He found another piece of beach glass—pale green, rounded smooth—and slipped it into the same pocket as the blue lure. Small talismans against the growing certainty that nothing would ever be found.

Around eleven he heard it.

A soft metallic bump against wood.

He froze mid-step on the path back up to the house. The sound came again—gentle, rhythmic, like a boat nudging its mooring in a light chop.

Elias ran.

He took the stone steps two at a time, breath burning in his throat, boots slipping on wet moss. When he reached the dock the world tilted.

The skiff was there.

Fourteen feet of dull aluminum, green hull streaked with salt, tied to the cleat exactly as Mara always tied it: bow line looped twice, finished with a perfect figure-eight knot. The oars were stowed parallel in the thwarts. The tackle box sat latched in its usual place forward. The small cooler—Mara's cooler—rested midships, lid still clipped shut. A half-empty bottle of water rolled lazily in the bilge with each tiny swell, the plastic crinkling softly.

No blood. No torn fabric. No overturned seat. No sign of anything except perfect, impossible order.

Elias stepped onto the dock planks. They creaked under his weight. He crouched beside the boat, fingers trembling as he traced the bow line. The knot was hers—same slight asymmetry in the upper loop she always left because she tied it fast when she was excited about a bite. He tugged it once. It held fast.

He climbed aboard.

The aluminum was cold through his jeans. He opened the cooler first: the thermos still inside, coffee long gone cold; two wax-paper-wrapped sandwiches, peanut butter and banana, uneaten; the fleece she'd packed "just in case." He lifted the tackle box lid. Lures, hooks, sinkers—all in their compartments. One empty spot where the silver mackerel jig should have been. The one she'd been tying on when she left.

He sat on the center thwart and stared at his hands. They looked foreign—red-knuckled, salt-cracked. He pressed his palms to his eyes until colors burst behind the lids.

When he looked up again, the coast guard cutter was already rounding the point.

Ruiz arrived first, boots heavy on the planks. Behind him, two crewmen in orange exposure suits, then Cal and another fisherman whose name Elias could never remember. They stopped at the edge of the dock, staring.

"Jesus," Cal breathed.

Ruiz crouched beside the boat, studied the knot, the oars, the cooler. He didn't touch anything at first. Then he lifted the bow line, examined the figure-eight, let it drop back into place.

"Same as the others," he said quietly. Not to Elias. To himself.

They photographed everything. Measured. Noted. The VHF crackled with updates to the station. Elias stood on the dock and answered questions in a voice that sounded borrowed from someone else. Yes, that was her knot. Yes, that was her cooler. Yes, that was the same water bottle she'd taken with her.

They searched the boat again—bilge, under the thwarts, inside the tackle box a second time. Nothing new. No note. No message. No body.

Ruiz put a hand on Elias's shoulder before he left. The grip was firm, brief.

"We'll keep looking," he said. "But this… this changes the profile."

Elias nodded. He didn't ask what the new profile was. He already knew.

The boats left. The dock emptied. The skiff rocked gently against the pilings, bow line creaking once, softly.

Elias stayed until the sun slid behind the western headland and the cold began to bite through his sweater. Then he climbed the steps, entered the lighthouse, closed the door behind him.

Inside, the house smelled stale—old coffee, congealed stew, the faint metallic edge of unlit oil lamps. He lit the stove anyway, more for light than heat. The flame bloomed orange, threw shadows across the pine floor.

He went to the south window.

She was there.

Not Mara.

The woman with the long blonde hair stood just inside the glass, facing the sea. Moonlight—thin, newly arrived—caught in the strands and turned them almost silver. She wore something pale and old-fashioned, high-collared, sleeves falling past her wrists. Her hands were folded at her waist. She did not move.

Elias stepped closer. The floorboard creaked under his boot—the three-note pattern near the bookshelf. The figure did not flinch.

"Who are you?" he asked. His voice cracked on the last word.

She turned slowly.

Her face was half-shadow, but the eyes were visible—wide-set, pale as sea glass. Not hazel. Not warm. They regarded him without surprise, without fear.

"You came back," she said.

The voice was soft, layered, as though spoken underwater and carried on the tide. It filled the room without effort.

Elias's throat closed. "That's not my wife."

"No," the woman said. "But she is here."

He took another step. The glass between them fogged with his breath.

"Where?"

She lifted one hand—long fingers, pale nails—and pressed her palm to the inside of the window. On Elias's side, frost bloomed around his own hand when he mirrored the gesture without thinking. The cold burned.

"The sea keeps what it takes," she said. "Until it decides to give something else instead."

Elias stared at the place where their palms almost touched. "Give her back."

The woman tilted her head. A faint smile moved across her lips—small, sad, knowing.

"I am not the one who decides," she said. "But I can show you where to ask."

She stepped back.

The silhouette blurred at the edges, hair lifting as though in an underwater current. Then she was gone—dissolved into the dark beyond the glass.

Elias stood there until his hand went numb against the window.

Behind him, the keeper's logs waited on the table. The town file from the library lay beside them, edges curling.

He turned slowly.

Tomorrow he would go back into town.

Tomorrow he would read every page again.

Tomorrow he would ask the lighthouse itself.

For now, he sank into the chair by the stove, staring at the south window where nothing but moonlight remained.

The skiff bumped once more against the dock below—soft, patient, waiting.

The lighthouse settled around him with a long, low sigh.

CHAPTER

Seven

The Whispering Window

Elias did not sleep that night.

He sat in the chair by the woodstove until the embers dulled to a faint orange pulse, then moved to the couch where the cushions still held the faint imprint of Mara's body from the last time they'd curled there together watching the fire. The skiff's return had left a hollow ringing in his ears, like the aftermath of a bell struck too hard. Every small sound in the lighthouse—the creak of cooling iron, the drip of condensation from a high window, the soft bump of the boat against the dock below—felt amplified, personal.

He kept the south window in his peripheral vision. Moonlight slanted across the floor in pale bars. He waited for her to reappear.

She did not.

Around three in the morning he rose, stiff and cold, and climbed the spiral stairs to the lantern room. The fairy lights still burned low; he had not turned them off since the storm began. Their amber glow made the curved glass look like the inside of an enormous seashell. He stood at the railing, palms on the cold iron, staring down at the dock. The skiff floated there, motionless now that the tide had turned, bow line taut and perfect.

He whispered her name into the dark.

"Mara."

The word fell flat. No echo. No answer.

He stayed until the first gray light seeped into the sky, then descended again. Coffee. Toast he could not eat. The keeper's logs waited on the table like patients in a waiting room. He opened the one from Thomas Voss, read the same entry for the tenth time, then the eleventh.

She is gone.

The words had begun to feel like a personal address.

By mid-morning the search boats were out again, though fewer. Two lobster boats and the cutter, running long parallel lines farther offshore. Elias watched from the catwalk until his eyes burned, then came down and drove into town.

The library smelled of old paper and lemon polish. Mrs. Hargrove looked up from her desk as the bell above the door jingled. Her face softened when she saw him—pity mixed with something sharper, almost wary.

"You're back," she said.

"I need more," Elias told her. "Anything. Photographs. Letters. Town meeting minutes. Whatever you have on the keepers' wives."

She studied him a long moment, then nodded once. "Sit."

She disappeared into the back room and returned with a cardboard box tied with cotton string. Dust puffed into the air when she set it on the table. Inside: loose photographs in sepia and faded black-and-white, a few handwritten letters in envelopes brittle with age, a slim ledger of town council notes from the 1920s and 1950s.

He started with the photographs.

Abigail Hale stared out from 1880—dark hair pinned severely, high collar, eyes direct and slightly sad. Lillian Voss next, 1923: long pale hair loose over her shoulders, almost defiant in the way she met the camera. Eleanor Price, 1957: shorter hair, modern permanent wave, but the same watchful expression.

None of them looked like Mara.

But all of them looked like the woman at the window.

He turned the photographs over. Faded pencil notes on the backs.

Abigail, before the January storm.

Lillian, summer she disappeared.

Eleanor, last known photograph, October.

He copied every detail into his notebook: dates, clothing, small background elements—a brass telescope on a tripod, a lobster pot in the foreground, the same south window behind each woman.

Mrs. Hargrove watched him without speaking.

When he reached the letters, his hands shook.

One from Thomas Voss to the town council, dated August 1923:

The house remembers. She stands at the window still. I hear her skirts on the stairs at night. I do not sleep.

Another, from Eleanor Price's husband, undated but context placed it in late 1957:

She says the sea gave her something back. I do not know what. I see her sometimes, but it is not her.

Elias closed the box slowly.

"Thank you," he said.

Mrs. Hargrove leaned forward. "Be careful what you ask the house, Elias. Some questions only make it louder."

He drove home in silence, notebook heavy on the passenger seat.

That night the figure returned.

She stood at the window as before, long hair catching moonlight like spun glass. Elias approached slowly, boots soft on the floorboards.

"You said you could show me where to ask," he said.

She turned. The movement was fluid, almost liquid.

"You already know where," she answered. Her voice carried the same submerged quality—soft, echoing faintly.

"The sea?"

She inclined her head. "And the place that listens to it."

He pressed his palm to the glass again. Frost spidered outward.

"Tell me your name."

"Lillian," she said.

The name landed like a stone in still water.

"You're not real," he whispered.

"I was once." She lifted her hand to mirror his again. "Now I am kept."

"By what?"

"By what was promised."

Elias felt the cold seep through the glass into his bones. "What was promised?"

She smiled—small, sorrowful. "A trade. One for one. The sea does not take without balance."

He stared at her pale eyes. "Give her back."

"I cannot," Lillian said. "But you can ask. At the place where the light used to burn."

She stepped back. Her form thinned, hair lifting as though stirred by an invisible tide.

"Wait—"

She dissolved.

Elias stood with his hand still on the glass long after she was gone.

The next morning he climbed to the lantern room in daylight for the first time since Mara vanished. The old Fresnel lens was gone—removed decades ago when the light was decommissioned—but the brass fittings remained, tarnished green. He ran his fingers over the mechanism where the lamp once turned.

Nothing happened.

He descended, opened the logs again, searched for references to the lantern itself.

In Josiah Hale's earliest entries:

The light must burn true. If it falters, the sea grows restless.

In Thomas Voss:

Lillian says the light calls things back. Or calls them in.

Elias closed the book.

He looked toward the south window.

Tonight, he decided.

Tonight he would ask.

Eight

The Lantern's Shadow

The seventh day passed in a haze of waiting.

The search boats were down to one—the cutter making wide, mechanical sweeps while the village volunteers had begun to drift back to their own lives. Elias no longer went down to the dock to watch them. He stayed inside, moving between the kitchen, the table of logs, and the south window. He ate nothing but coffee and the occasional cracker that tasted like cardboard.

He cleaned the lantern room instead.

He wiped every pane of the curved glass with vinegar and newspaper until it shone. He polished the brass fittings until they gleamed dull gold. He strung fresh batteries into the old marine lantern he'd found in the cellar—a small, battery-powered beacon meant for boats—and set it on the pedestal where the Fresnel once stood.

He did not light it yet.

He waited for dark.

When night came, the house felt different—tighter, as though the walls had drawn closer. The wind was light, almost absent; the sea murmured steadily below. Elias carried the marine lantern up the spiral stairs, each step deliberate. The fairy lights were off tonight; he wanted no competing glow.

He set the lantern on the pedestal, thumbed the switch.

A white beam cut through the dark, narrow and bright, sweeping slowly across the water as he turned the handle by hand. It was not the great revolving light of old—just a steady pulse—but it felt like something waking.

He stood at the railing, beam sweeping, voice low.

"Mara."

Nothing.

He spoke again, louder.

"If you're here—if you can hear me—come back."

The beam swept. The sea answered with its usual sigh.

He turned to the south window inside the lantern room.

Lillian was there.

She stood closer tonight, almost within arm's reach if the glass were not between them. Her pale dress moved faintly, as though stirred by breath.

"You lit the light," she said.

"I'm asking," Elias told her.

She studied him. "Asking is not enough."

"Then what is?"

"Giving."

He felt the word like a slap. "I've given everything."

"Not yet."

She lifted her hand to the glass. Elias mirrored her without hesitation. The frost came faster this time, crawling up his wrist.

"The sea took because something was owed," Lillian said. "Long ago. A promise made in storm and blood. One wife for the light. One life to keep the ships safe. The bargain was broken when the light went out."

Elias's breath fogged the space between their palms.

"And now?"

"Now it wants balance again."

He stared into her pale eyes. "I won't give another life."

"Not yours," she said softly. "Hers is already taken. But something else. A memory. A promise. A piece of you."

He felt the cold travel up his arm, into his chest.

"What piece?"

She smiled—gentle, terrible. "The part that still believes she will come back unchanged."

Elias jerked his hand away. The frost cracked.

Lillian's form wavered.

"Wait—"

"Light the lantern every night," she said. "Ask every night. But know that each time you ask, you give a little more."

She faded.

Elias stood in the sweeping beam, heart hammering.

He left the lantern burning.

All night.

CHAPTER

Nine

The Slow Unraveling

The eighth day dawned colder.

Elias woke on the iron bed in the lantern room, clothes rumpled, throat raw from whispering into the dark. The marine lantern still glowed weakly—batteries nearly spent. He switched it off, carried it downstairs, recharged it with the solar panel on the catwalk.

He did not speak to anyone.

The coast guard called once. Ruiz's voice on the VHF: routine check-in, no new leads, weather forecast deteriorating again by weekend. Elias answered in monosyllables.

He spent the day in the cellar.

He moved boxes, swept dust from stone arches, searched for anything hidden. Behind a stack of lobster traps he found a small iron box, rusted shut. Inside: a tarnished silver locket, a folded letter on brittle paper, a single photograph of a woman who was not Abigail, not Lillian, not Eleanor—but who had the same pale hair, the same watchful eyes. Tucked beside the letter was a small glass vial stoppered with wax, containing seawater that had never settled—tiny motes of light drifting inside, suspended, never sinking. Elias stared at the motes a moment, then closed the box and told himself it was only a curiosity.

The letter was undated, ink faded:

The bargain must be renewed. One light for one life. The sea will not wait forever.

He carried the box upstairs, set it on the table beside the logs.

That night he lit the lantern again.

He stood at the railing, beam sweeping the black water.

"Mara. If you can hear me. I'm trying."

Lillian appeared at the window below.

She did not speak at first. Just watched him.

When he descended to the main floor, she was waiting.

"You are giving," she said.

"I don't feel it."

"You will."

He pressed his palm to the glass. No frost this time—just cold.

"What happens if I stop asking?"

"The sea keeps her."

"And if I keep asking?"

"You become part of the bargain."

Elias felt something shift inside his chest—small, almost imperceptible. A loosening.

He looked at her pale face.

"Show me her."

Lillian tilted her head. "Not yet."

"When?"

"When you have nothing left to hold back."

She stepped back, dissolved.

Elias stood alone.

He lit the lantern every night after that.

Each dawn he felt a little thinner.

Each night the figure watched a little closer.

The suspense coiled tighter.

The sea waited.

Ten

The First Promise

Elias lit the lantern again that night, the ninth since the skiff had returned.

The marine beacon's beam swept the black water in slow, mechanical arcs—narrow, white, insistent. He stood at the catwalk railing, wind tugging at his sweater, the iron cold enough to bite through the wool into his palms. Below, the sea murmured its endless rhythm, each wave sighing against the rocks as though it knew he was listening. The fairy lights were dark; he wanted nothing to soften the edge of what he asked.

"Mara," he said into the dark. "If you're out there… if you can still hear me… I'm still trying."

The beam swept. The sea gave nothing back.

He descended the spiral stairs, each step creaking its familiar descending scale, the sound now laced with something heavier, like the house itself exhaling in weary sympathy. The kitchen smelled of stale coffee and the faint metallic tang of the woodstove he had not bothered to relight. He poured the last of the cold brew into a mug anyway, the liquid bitter on his tongue, and carried it to the south window.

Lillian waited.

She stood closer tonight—close enough that the pale fabric of her high-collared dress seemed to press against the inside of the glass. Her long blonde hair drifted slowly, as though moved by a current only she could feel. The pale eyes met his without blinking.

"You are thinner," she said. The voice still carried that submerged echo, soft and layered.

"I'm giving," Elias answered. His own voice sounded scraped raw. "Like you said."

She inclined her head. Moonlight silvered the strands of hair that framed her face. "The bargain requires more than light. It requires understanding."

He set the mug on the windowsill. The ceramic clinked against wood. "Then tell me where it began."

Lillian's smile was small, sorrowful, almost tender. "Not I. The house remembers. But it will not speak unless you make it."

She lifted one hand. No frost this time—just a faint pressure against the glass, as though she were pushing the memory toward him rather than touching him. The pane misted briefly, not with his breath but with something older, something that smelled suddenly of whale oil and wet wool and the sharp ozone of a storm that had never truly ended.

"Begin at the beginning," she whispered.

Then she was gone, dissolved into shadow so cleanly that the window looked ordinary again, reflecting only his own hollow-eyed face.

Elias stood there until the coffee grew a skin on its surface. When he finally turned away, the keeper's logs no longer felt sufficient. They began in 1879—too late. The bargain, whatever it was, had been struck the year the lighthouse first rose from the rocks.

He slept fitfully on the couch, dreams tangled with sweeping beams and pale hair and the sound of a woman's skirts brushing iron stairs. At dawn he drove into town again, the notebook open on the passenger seat, the silver locket from the cellar box heavy in his coat pocket.

The county historical society occupied a narrow brick building behind the library, its windows fogged with age. The archivist—a wiry woman named Ruth with steel-gray hair pinned in a tight bun—recognized him the moment he stepped inside. The bell above the door gave a single, mournful chime.

"You're the one at Blackthorn," she said without preamble. Her voice was dry as old paper. "I heard about your wife. I'm sorry."

Elias set the locket on the counter. The silver had tarnished to a dull gray; the clasp was fused shut. "This was in the cellar. There was a letter with it. Something about a bargain. A light for a life."

Ruth's eyes sharpened. She did not touch the locket at first. Instead she studied his face—sunken cheeks, the new lines around his mouth, the way his hands trembled slightly when he withdrew them.

"Most people who come asking about Blackthorn leave before they find this," she said quietly. "You're still here."

She unlocked a tall metal cabinet in the back room and returned with a flat, acid-free box. Inside lay a single leather-bound journal, its cover cracked and stained with what might have been seawater or blood or both. The first page was dated 14 October 1878—two weeks before the lighthouse was officially commissioned.

Captain Josiah Hale's hand. But different from the logs upstairs. Wilder. The ink darker, the letters slanted as though written in wind.

Elias read aloud, voice low:

"The gale came without warning. Three ships on the reef. I lit the lamp with the last of the whale oil, but the wind took the flame twice. Men drowned within sight of the light. That night, with the storm still howling, I walked the catwalk and made a promise to whatever listens when the light fails. One life to keep the beacon burning. One wife for every ship saved. The sea answered. The oil burned true until dawn. Abigail slept through it all. I have not told her."

Ruth watched him without interrupting. The room smelled of dust and old ink and the faint, persistent brine that seemed to follow him everywhere now.

He turned the page. The entries grew shorter, more fevered.

"17 October – The light holds. Two more ships passed safely. But Abigail complains of cold at the south window. She says she hears waves inside the walls."

"22 October – The sea sent a token. A single strand of pale hair on the lantern pedestal. Not Abigail's. I burned it. The flame turned blue."

"5 November – The bargain is sealed. I felt it in my chest when I lit the lamp tonight—like a hook set deep. Abigail will never know. The light must burn forever."

Elias closed the journal slowly. His fingers left faint prints on the leather. The locket on the counter seemed to pulse in the dim light.

Ruth finally spoke. "There were earlier keepers—unofficial ones—before the government took over. Hale wasn't the first to stand on those rocks. But he was the first to bargain. The town records mention a 'pact with the tide' in the old ledgers. They stopped writing about it after 1881. After Abigail."

Elias's throat tightened. "What happened in 1881?"

Ruth hesitated. Then she pulled a second, thinner folder from the cabinet. A single yellowed newspaper clipping, brittle as dead leaves.

LIGHTHOUSE WIFE LOST IN SUDDEN SQUALL – BOAT RETURNED EMPTY

The photograph beneath showed Abigail Hale, dark hair, direct eyes. But in the margin, in Hale's own cramped hand: The sea kept its promise. The light still burns.

Elias stared until the words blurred.

Ruth closed the folder gently. "Some places don't forget debts, Mr. Callahan. Blackthorn Light was never just a lighthouse. It was a bargain made in blood and storm. When the government decommissioned the lamp in 1942, the debt went unpaid. The sea has been waiting ever since."

He drove home with the journal on the seat beside him, the locket burning a cold circle against his chest. The wind had risen again by the time he reached the point—low moans that found every crack in the tower walls.

That night he lit the lantern earlier.

He stood at the catwalk, beam sweeping, and spoke directly to the dark.

"I know what you took. I know why."

Lillian appeared at the south window below, closer still—her face almost touching the glass from the inside.

"You have seen the beginning," she said. Her voice carried the crash of waves now, faint but unmistakable.

"Tell me the end," Elias demanded. "How do I break it?"

She shook her head slowly. "There is no breaking. Only renewing."

He descended the stairs two at a time. When he reached the window she was waiting, palm already pressed to the glass.

"The first promise was one wife," she whispered. "To keep the light burning for every ship that would have wrecked. Hale gave Abigail. The sea gave safety. When the light went out, the debt doubled. Two wives. Then three. Now four."

Elias felt the hook she had spoken of—something sharp and ancient settling deeper behind his ribs.

"Mara is the fourth?"

Lillian's pale eyes softened with something almost like pity. "She is the payment. Unless you offer something else in her place."

"What?"

"Your own light," she said. "The part of you that still hopes. Give that, and the sea may release what it holds."

Elias pressed his hand to the glass opposite hers. This time the frost came fast and vicious, crawling up his arm like living ice. The cold burned all the way to his shoulder.

"I won't," he said through gritted teeth.

Lillian smiled—small, ancient, inevitable.

"Then the lantern must burn brighter," she said. "And you must keep asking. Until there is nothing left of you to give."

She stepped back. Her form thinned, but not before he saw it—a flicker behind her, deeper in the glass, a shadow with chestnut hair and hazel eyes that reached one hand toward him before vanishing.

Mara.

Just for an instant.

Elias staggered back from the window, heart slamming against his ribs.

The journal lay open on the table. The first promise stared up at him in Josiah Hale's desperate hand.

He lit the lantern again at midnight, even though the batteries were failing.

He stood in the sweeping beam and whispered into the wind until his voice gave out.

The sea listened.

The house listened.

And somewhere beneath the waves, something shifted—closer now, patient, still hungry.

CHAPTER

Eleven

The Hook Deepens

Elias did not leave the lantern room that night.

He stayed on the catwalk long after the beam had begun to flicker—batteries dying again, the light stuttering like a heartbeat losing rhythm. The wind had dropped to almost nothing; the sea lay flat and black, reflecting the thin moon in broken silver shards. He leaned against the railing until his arms went numb, whispering the same plea over and over until the words lost shape and became only breath.

"Mara. Mara. Mara."

No answer came from the water. No running light appeared. No pale hand reached up from the depths.

When the beam finally failed, he carried the lantern downstairs, set it on the kitchen table beside the open journal. The pages had begun to feel warm under his fingers, as though the ink still carried the heat of Josiah Hale's desperation. He read the entry from 5 November 1878 again, tracing the words with a fingertip that left faint sweat marks on the paper.

The bargain is sealed. I felt it in my chest when I lit the lamp tonight—like a hook set deep.

He pressed his palm to his own sternum. There it was: a small, persistent pressure, not quite pain, not quite ache—something that had settled behind his ribs the night the skiff returned and had grown heavier with each passing day. It tugged when he thought of Mara's laugh, when he remembered the way her hazel eyes crinkled at the corners. It tightened when he looked at the south window.

He did not sleep.

At dawn he rose, joints stiff, eyes gritty, and walked the shoreline again. The shingle was cold under his bare feet—he had forgotten boots. The tide had left a thin line of foam and broken shells; among them lay a single chestnut strand of hair, still damp, curled like a question mark. He picked it up between thumb and forefinger. It smelled faintly of her shampoo—vanilla and sea salt.

He carried it back to the house, placed it beside the silver locket on the table. The two hairs—one dark, one pale—lay side by side like opposing witnesses.

He made no coffee that morning. The stove remained cold. Instead he opened Ruth's folder again, spread the photographs across the pine surface. Abigail. Lillian. Eleanor. And now Mara's face in his mind, superimposed over each of them. He stared until the images blurred into one composite woman—dark hair bleeding into pale, hazel eyes fading to sea-glass gray.

The pressure in his chest pulsed once, sharply.

He drove into town again that afternoon, though he had no clear plan. The Subaru rattled over frost-heaved roads; the heater blew lukewarm air that smelled faintly of burnt dust. He parked outside the historical society and sat in the car for ten minutes, hands on the wheel, staring at the brick building without moving.

When he finally entered, Ruth was waiting at the counter as though she had expected him.

"You look worse," she said plainly.

He set the silver locket down between them. "There's more in here. I can feel it."

Ruth did not open it. She studied his face instead—the new hollows under his eyes, the way his shoulders curved inward as though protecting something fragile inside.

"Come with me," she said.

She led him through a narrow door behind the counter, down a short flight of stairs into a basement room that smelled of damp stone and mildew. A single bare bulb hung from the ceiling.

Against the far wall stood a tall wooden cabinet, its doors carved with faint nautical motifs—anchors, ropes, stylized waves.

Ruth produced a brass key from her pocket and unlocked it.

Inside, on the middle shelf, rested a small iron strongbox—smaller than the one Elias had found in the cellar, its lid etched with the same words that had appeared in Hale's journal: One light for one life.

She lifted it carefully, set it on a scarred worktable, and stepped back.

"I've never opened it," she said. "No one has, not in my lifetime. My predecessor told me it was sealed for a reason. But you're the first person in sixty years who's asked the right questions."

Elias's hand hovered over the lid. The metal was cold, almost burning. When he touched it, the hook in his chest twisted—once, hard.

He lifted the lid.

Inside lay a single sheet of parchment, folded once, edges frayed. Beside it, the same small glass vial stoppered with wax, containing seawater that had never settled—tiny motes of light drifting inside, suspended, never sinking.

He unfolded the parchment with trembling fingers.

The handwriting was not Hale's. Older. Spidery. Dated 14 October 1878—the same night as Hale's first desperate entry.

To whoever lights the lamp after me:

The sea spoke first. I was alone on the point, the gale tearing the world apart, three ships already broken on the rocks below. I had no oil left. The wick was dry. In my terror I cried out— not to God, but to the water itself. It answered. A voice from the deep, calm as a held breath. It said: Give me one life, and I will keep the light burning. One wife for every soul saved from this point forward. I swore it on my own blood. The oil appeared in the reservoir as though poured from nowhere. The flame caught and held against the wind. The ships that came after passed safely.

But the sea does not forget. When the lamp was taken away in 1942, the debt remained. It waits for renewal. It will take what was promised—four times now, because four keepers failed to keep the bargain after me. The fifth must pay in full, or the debt will never close.

The vial contains the first promise—seawater from that night. Break it, and the bargain ends. Keep it sealed, and the light must burn again, or the sea will claim what it is owed.

Choose wisely. The hook is already set.

—E. Blackthorn, First Watcher

Elias stared at the signature. Blackthorn. The point itself had signed the letter.

He looked at Ruth. "Who was E. Blackthorn?"

"No one knows," she said quietly. "Not a man. Not a woman. Just the name on the earliest deed for the land. Some say it wasn't a person at all. Just the place naming itself."

Elias lifted the vial. The liquid inside moved slowly, the tiny lights pulsing in time with his heartbeat. Or perhaps with the hook in his chest.

He closed the strongbox. The lid clicked shut with a sound like a lock turning.

"I'm not breaking it yet," he said.

Ruth nodded once, unsurprised. "Then you'd better keep the lantern burning."

He drove home in silence, the strongbox on the passenger seat beside him.

That night he carried the marine lantern and the vial up to the lantern room together.

He lit the beam. It swept the dark water.

He set the vial on the pedestal beside it.

He spoke to the empty room.

"I know who made the promise. I know what it cost. I know it's still open."

Lillian did not appear at the window.

Instead, the pressure in his chest deepened—slowly, deliberately, like a hand closing around his heart.

He stayed in the sweeping light until the batteries died again.

When the beam failed, the vial glowed faintly from within— small, cold, persistent.

The sea had noticed.

The hook had tightened.

And somewhere beneath the waves, something older than Hale, older than the lighthouse itself, began to stir.

Twelve

The Weight of Light

The vial glowed all night.

Not brightly—only a faint, cold luminescence that pulsed in slow rhythm with the distant breakers. Elias left it on the lantern-room pedestal beside the dead marine beacon, unwilling to carry it downstairs, unwilling to let it out of sight. He sat on the iron bed with his back against the curved glass, knees drawn up, watching the tiny motes inside the glass drift and circle like captive stars. Each time one flared brighter, the hook behind his ribs gave a corresponding tug—sharp enough now to make him catch his breath.

He did not speak to the empty room. He had nothing new to say.

At some point before dawn he must have dozed, because he woke to pale gray light filling the lantern room and the vial no longer glowing. The seawater inside looked ordinary again—murky, still, unremarkable. He lifted it carefully, turned it in his fingers. The wax stopper remained intact; no crack, no leak. Yet the pressure in his chest had not eased. If anything, it had settled deeper, like an anchor finding bottom.

He carried the vial downstairs.

The kitchen was colder than it should have been. Frost rimed the inside of the south window even though the woodstove had not been lit in days. Elias set the vial on the table beside Mara's single chestnut hair and the pale strand from the beach. The three objects lay in a loose triangle: dark hair, pale hair, glowing promise. He stared at them until his eyes watered.

He made no breakfast. Instead he opened Josiah Hale's journal to the entry dated 22 October 1878—the one about the first token.

A single strand of pale hair on the lantern pedestal. Not Abigail's. I burned it. The flame turned blue.

Elias looked at the pale strand on the table. His hand moved before he could think better of it. He picked it up, carried it to the woodstove, opened the door. Embers from two nights ago still smoldered faintly. He dropped the hair onto the coals.

It did not burn.

It curled once, slowly, then lay still—unscorched, untouched. The embers flared blue for half a second, bright enough to sting his eyes, then dulled again to ordinary orange.

He closed the stove door with a soft clang.

The hook twisted—once, deliberately.

He exhaled through his teeth and went outside.

The morning was windless, the sky the color of tarnished silver. The skiff floated at the dock exactly as it had for days—bow line perfect, no drift, no wear on the rope. He walked down the stone steps anyway, boots crunching on frost-rimed gravel. When he reached the planks he crouched beside the boat and laid his palm on the gunwale.

The aluminum was warm.

Not hot. Not feverish. Just… body temperature. As though someone had been sitting there moments before he arrived.

He jerked his hand back.

The water bottle still rolled gently in the bilge. He reached in, lifted it. The plastic was warm too. He unscrewed the cap. Inside, the water moved—small, slow swirls that had not been there yesterday. He tilted the bottle; a single drop clung to the rim, trembled, then fell back inside without spilling.

He screwed the cap on again, set the bottle carefully on the thwart.

When he looked up, Lillian stood at the end of the dock.

Not in the window. Not a reflection. Solid—or as solid as mist can be—standing on the last plank, bare feet inches above the wet wood. Her pale dress hung motionless despite the faint breeze that had begun to stir. Long blonde hair drifted behind her like seaweed in a gentle current.

Elias stood slowly.

"You're here," he said.

"I am always here," she answered. "You are only now seeing."

He took one step toward her. The dock creaked under his weight.

"The vial," he said. "What happens if I break it?"

Her pale eyes regarded him without blinking. "The debt ends. The sea forgets. Mara returns."

The words landed like stones in still water. Ripples moved through him—hope, terror, disbelief.

"Unchanged?"

Lillian's smile was small, almost pitying. "The sea does not return things unchanged."

He felt the hook shift again—deeper this time, scraping against bone.

"What does she become?"

"Something the sea has kept," Lillian said softly. "Something that remembers the dark. Something that will always hear the tide."

Elias looked down at the skiff. The water bottle had stopped rolling. The surface inside was perfectly still now.

"I won't do that to her," he said.

"Then you must keep the bargain yourself."

He met her gaze. "How?"

"Light the lantern every night. Speak her name every night. Give a piece of yourself every night—until there is nothing left to give."

"And then?"

"Then the sea may decide the debt is paid another way."

She stepped backward—once, twice—until her heels were over the edge of the dock. She did not fall. She simply faded into the gray air above the water, hair trailing last like smoke.

Elias stood alone on the dock until the cold drove him back inside.

That afternoon he recharged the marine lantern's batteries with the solar panel on the catwalk. The sun was thin, reluctant; the charge took longer than usual. While he waited he opened the strongbox again, studied the vial more closely. The motes inside had begun to cluster—small constellations that formed and dissolved, almost like shapes trying to be letters.

He closed the box.

He did not drive into town.

He stayed in the lighthouse, moving from room to room, touching things Mara had touched—the chipped mug she always used for tea, the clay pot of rosemary on the sill that had begun to wilt, the record player still set to the last album they'd played together. He did not play it. He only ran his fingers over the worn label.

Night came early.

He carried the lantern and the vial back to the lantern room.

He lit the beam. It swept the black water—stronger tonight, the batteries fresh.

He set the vial beside it.

He spoke her name into the sweeping light.

"Mara."

The hook answered—slow, grinding pressure that made his vision narrow for a second.

He stayed there until the beam began to dim again.

When he descended to the south window, Lillian was waiting—closer than ever, her palm already pressed to the glass.

"You gave tonight," she said.

"I said her name."

"That is enough. For now."

He mirrored her hand. No frost. Just cold glass and the faint warmth of his own skin.

"Show me her again," he said.

Lillian tilted her head. "You are not ready."

"I'm ready."

She studied him a long moment. Then she stepped sideways—not disappearing, but moving deeper into the reflection of the room behind the glass.

And there, in the shadowed corner of that reflected lantern room, stood Mara.

Chestnut hair loose over her shoulders. Hazel eyes wide, searching. She wore the green hoodie she had fished in, sleeves pushed up, yellow slicker half-unzipped. Her lips moved—soundless, urgent—but no words came through the glass.

Elias pressed both hands to the pane.

"Mara!"

Her head turned toward his voice. Recognition flickered in her eyes—brief, bright, heartbreaking. She reached out one hand.

The image fractured.

Lillian stepped back into the foreground. Mara vanished behind her like smoke.

"You saw," Lillian said quietly.

Elias's knees buckled. He caught himself on the windowsill.

"She's alive," he whispered.

"She is kept," Lillian corrected. "Alive is not the same as free."

He stared at the empty glass. "How do I get her out?"

"Give more," Lillian said. "Or break the vial. But know this: once broken, the sea will demand its balance in full. Four lives—or one very great sacrifice."

She began to fade.

"Wait—please—"

"Light tomorrow," she said. "And give again."

Gone.

Elias sank to the floor, back against the wall, staring at the south window where nothing remained but his own reflection—thinner, grayer, eyes hollowed by something that was no longer only grief.

The hook pulsed steadily now.

A metronome.

Counting down.

CHAPTER

Thirteen

Pale at the Edges

Dawn came thin and reluctant, the kind of light that barely pushes back the dark before retreating again. Elias woke on the floor of the lantern room, cheek pressed to the cold iron grating, one arm numb beneath him. The vial still sat on the pedestal—seawater motionless now, motes settled at the bottom like fine silt. The marine lantern's beam had died hours earlier; the room smelled faintly of hot metal and ozone.

He pushed himself up slowly. His joints protested with small, sharp pops. When he rubbed his face, his fingers encountered stubble that felt coarser than yesterday, and something else—strands of hair falling across his forehead that caught the gray light wrong. He froze.

He crossed to the curved glass, leaned close enough that his breath fogged it, and parted his own hair with trembling fingers.

A thin streak—pale as winter surf—ran from his left temple back toward the crown. Not gray. Not white. The same luminous platinum that drifted behind Lillian's head every night. It was narrow, no wider than a finger's width, but unmistakable.

He stared until his reflection blurred.

The hook in his chest gave a slow, satisfied twist.

He descended the spiral stairs without turning on any lights. The house felt heavier this morning, the air thicker, as though the walls had absorbed the night's cold and were now exhaling it back into the rooms. In the kitchen he filled the kettle from the tap, set it on the stove, lit the burner with hands that shook only slightly. Routine. Anchor. He needed anchors.

While the water heated he stood at the south window, staring at the empty glass. No silhouette. No pale dress. Just frost still clinging to the lower panes in delicate fern patterns. He pressed a fingertip to one frond; it melted under his touch, leaving a clear droplet that ran down the glass like a tear.

The kettle whistled. He poured the water over coffee grounds in the old percolator, watched the dark bloom upward. The scent was bitter, grounding. He poured a mug, carried it to the table, sat.

The chestnut hair—Mara's—still lay beside the pale one. The vial between them. He reached for the dark strand first, lifted it to the light. It caught the weak sun and gleamed warm brown, almost red at the edges. He brought it to his nose. Faint vanilla. Faint sea. Faint her.

He closed his eyes.

When he opened them again, the pale streak in his own hair brushed his eyelashes.

He set the strand down carefully.

He drank the coffee black. It scalded his tongue; he welcomed the small, real pain.

Mid-morning he went outside.

The skiff waited at the dock, unchanged—bow line perfect, water bottle still in the bilge. He did not touch it this time. Instead he walked the shoreline, boots sinking into wet shingle, eyes scanning for more tokens. He found none. Only broken shells, strands of weed, the occasional gull feather bleached white by salt and sun.

When he returned to the house, a truck was parked at the top of the path.

Cal—the fisherman with the gray beard and rope-knotted hands—leaned against the fender, arms crossed. He straightened when Elias approached.

"Thought I'd check on you," Cal said. His voice was rough, but not unkind. "Haven't seen you down at the dock in days. Coast Guard's scaled back to twice-weekly sweeps. Figured someone should make sure you're still breathing."

Elias stopped a few feet away. "I'm breathing."

Cal studied him—really looked. His eyes narrowed at the pale streak in Elias's hair, at the hollows under his eyes, the way his sweater hung looser on shoulders that had already begun to narrow.

"You look like hell, son."

Elias gave a small, humorless smile. "I feel like it."

Cal pushed off the truck. "Come on. I brought chowder. Real stuff—clams I dug myself yesterday. You can eat it or throw it at me, but you're eating something."

He didn't wait for an answer. He opened the passenger door, pulled out a large thermos and a paper bag that smelled of salt pork and thyme. Elias followed him inside without protest.

In the kitchen Cal set the food on the counter, unscrewed the thermos lid. Steam rose, carrying the rich, briny scent that made Elias's stomach clench with sudden, sharp hunger he hadn't felt in days.

Cal ladled chowder into a bowl he found in the cupboard—the same bowl Mara had used for cereal the morning she left. Elias stared at it.

"Sit," Cal said.

Elias sat.

He ate slowly at first, then faster. The heat spread through him, loosening something in his chest that wasn't the hook. For a few minutes the pressure eased.

Cal watched without speaking until the bowl was half-empty.

"You're not sleeping," Cal said finally. "You're not eating. And that—" He gestured vaguely toward Elias's hair. "—that ain't natural."

Elias set the spoon down. "It's part of it."

"Part of what?"

"The lighthouse. The bargain."

Cal's face tightened. He leaned forward, elbows on the table. "I've lived on this coast my whole life. Heard the stories. Hale's wife. Voss's. Price's. Folks say the place is cursed. I always said it was just bad luck and worse weather. But I've seen lights in that tower at night when no one's supposed to be here. And now you're here, and you're fading like the rest of them."

Elias looked at him. "You believe it?"

"I believe what I see," Cal said quietly. "And I see a man who's giving himself away piece by piece. Whatever you're doing up there—lighting that lantern, talking to windows—you're feeding something. And it's hungry."

Elias's hand went to his chest without thinking. The hook pulsed once, acknowledging.

"I saw her," he said. "Last night. Through the glass. She reached for me."

Cal exhaled through his nose. "And what did the blonde one say?"

Elias stared. "You know about her?"

"Old timers talk. Always a woman with pale hair at the window. Always after a wife goes missing. Folks used to leave offerings—flowers, coins, once a wedding ring—on the dock to keep her quiet. Didn't work."

Elias felt the room tilt slightly. "What do they say happens if you keep feeding it?"

Cal looked away, toward the south window. "You become part of the light. Or part of the sea. Either way, you stop being you."

Silence stretched between them.

Cal stood. "I'm not telling you to leave. But I'm telling you to eat. Sleep if you can. And think hard about what you're trading. Because once it's gone—" He tapped his own chest. "—it doesn't come back."

He left the rest of the chowder on the counter, clapped Elias once on the shoulder—firm, brief—and walked out. The truck rumbled away down the path.

Elias sat alone with the cooling soup.

That night he lit the lantern again.

The beam swept stronger—new batteries, fresh charge. He stood at the railing, vial in one hand, speaking her name into the wind.

"Mara."

The hook answered—deeper now, grinding against bone.

He descended to the south window.

Lillian waited, palm pressed to the glass.

"You gave more tonight," she said.

"I spoke her name."

"And you let the fisherman see."

Elias frowned. "That wasn't part of it."

"Everything is part of it now."

She stepped aside.

Mara appeared again—clearer this time. Her hoodie sleeve was torn at the cuff; salt crusted the fabric. Her hazel eyes locked on his. Her mouth moved again—faster, more urgent. He thought he could read the shape of his name on her lips.

He slammed his palm against the glass.

"Mara! I'm here!"

Her hand lifted—fingers splayed, reaching.

The image held longer than before—three heartbeats, four—then shattered like thin ice.

Lillian returned to the foreground.

"She hears you," she said softly. "But the sea holds tight."

Elias's voice cracked. "How much more do I have to give?"

"Until the hook is set so deep there is no pulling it free," Lillian answered. "Or until you break the vial. The choice is yours. But each night you wait, the sea claims another piece."

She began to fade.

"Wait—please—"

"Light tomorrow," she said. "And give again."

Gone.

Elias sank to his knees before the window, his forehead pressed to the cold glass.

Behind him, the vial on the table began to glow once more—slow, persistent, patient.

The streak in his hair caught the moonlight and shimmered.

The hook counted another beat.

Closer now.

Always closer.

Fourteen

The Gathering Dark

The pale streak had widened by morning.

Elias noticed it the moment he caught his reflection in the kettle's dull chrome as he filled it again. The platinum thread now ran from temple to crown in a broader swath—narrow still, but unmistakable, like frost creeping across glass overnight. He touched it with wet fingers; the strands felt colder than the rest of his hair, almost brittle. When he pulled one free, it came away without resistance, gleaming faintly in the weak kitchen light before he let it drift to the floor.

He did not sweep it up.

The vial on the table no longer waited for night. Its glow persisted into daylight—a soft, submarine blue that pulsed faintly even under the overcast sky pressing against the windows. The motes inside had organized themselves further: small spirals now, turning slowly, counterclockwise, like water draining through an unseen hole. Elias watched them for a long minute, coffee forgotten on the burner until it boiled over with a sharp hiss.

He turned off the flame, wiped the spill with the dish towel Mara had always folded into perfect squares. The fabric still carried a ghost of her scent—vanilla fading, salt lingering.

Outside, the wind had returned.

Not the screaming gale of the night she disappeared, but a low, steady moan that found every crack in the tower and whistled through it like breath across a bottle neck. The weathervane turned lazily, its scrape slower than usual, almost thoughtful. Elias stepped onto the landing, coatless, letting the cold sink into his skin. The sea looked heavier today—darker, slower-moving, as though it carried extra weight.

He walked down to the dock.

The skiff had shifted slightly—not enough to strain the line, but enough to notice. The bow pointed a fraction more seaward than yesterday. The water bottle in the bilge no longer rolled; it sat upright in the center, perfectly balanced, as though placed there by careful hands. Elias crouched, reached in, lifted it.

The plastic was warmer still—almost feverish. He unscrewed the cap again. The water inside moved—deliberate swirls now, forming small eddies that spun and collapsed. One eddy held shape longer than the others: a rough circle, like an open mouth trying to speak.

He capped it quickly, set it back.

When he straightened, Lillian stood on the water.

Not on the dock. Not on the rocks. On the surface itself—bare feet resting on the chop without sinking, dress hem trailing in the swells but never wetting. Her long blonde hair lifted in the wind like pale smoke. She did not approach; she simply waited, thirty feet out, eyes fixed on him.

Elias gripped the cleat until his knuckles whitened.

"What now?" he called.

Her voice carried over the water—soft, submerged, clear as though she stood beside him.

"You gave again last night. The streak is proof."

He touched the pale swath in his hair. "It's spreading."

"It will continue to spread," she said. "Each night you light the lantern, each time you speak her name, another piece of you becomes the sea's. Hair. Skin. Breath. Memory. Until you are pale as I am."

Elias felt the hook respond—slow grind, deeper scrape. His chest ached with it now, a constant pressure that made every breath feel borrowed.

"And Mara?" he asked.

Lillian tilted her head. "She feels it too. Every piece you give, the sea loosens its grip on her a fraction. But it takes from you to do so."

He stared at her. "Then why not just break the vial? End it?"

"Because the sea does not end things cleanly," she answered. "Break it, and the debt settles all at once. Four lives—or one complete surrender. You would not survive the taking."

Elias looked down at the skiff. The water bottle had tilted again, mouth pointing toward the open sea.

"I saw her clearer last night," he said. "She was trying to speak."

"She is closer to the surface now," Lillian confirmed. "But still beneath. The lantern calls her nearer. Your giving pulls her up."

He stepped onto the dock planks. They creaked under him—familiar three-note pattern.

"Show me more," he said.

Lillian did not answer with words. Instead she raised one hand, palm out. The wind stilled instantly. The waves flattened to glass. From the center of that sudden calm rose a faint shimmer—like heat rising off summer asphalt, but cold.

Mara appeared—not in reflection, not behind glass, but projected onto the water itself. A wavering image, translucent, overlaid on the surface like oil on a puddle. She stood in the same green hoodie, yellow slicker half-zipped, hair wet and plastered to her cheeks. Her hazel eyes were wide, searching the horizon. Her mouth opened and closed—no sound, but the shape was clearer now: Eli… Eli…

She reached both hands forward, fingers spread as though pressing against an invisible barrier. The image rippled with each wave that tried to reclaim the flatness.

Elias dropped to his knees on the dock.

"Mara!"

Her head snapped toward his voice. Recognition flared—bright, desperate. She pounded once on the invisible wall, the impact sending concentric rings outward across the water. The image held—five seconds, six—then fractured into foam as the wind returned and the sea remembered itself.

Lillian lowered her hand. The water roughened again.

"She heard you," she said quietly. "She is fighting."

Elias stayed on his knees, breath ragged. "How much longer?"

"Until you have no more to give," Lillian answered. "Or until you choose the breaking. But the sea grows impatient. The storm tomorrow will test what remains."

She began to sink—slowly, gracefully—hair trailing upward like pale kelp as the water closed over her head. Her eyes stayed on his until the last moment.

"Light the lantern tonight," she said, voice echoing from beneath the surface now. "And give more."

Then she was gone.

Elias remained on the dock until his knees went numb and the cold had seeped deep into his bones. When he finally stood, the pale streak in his hair had widened another fraction—visible even in the flat daylight.

He climbed the steps back to the house.

Inside, the vial's glow had strengthened—bright enough now to cast faint blue shadows across the pine floor. The motes spun faster, tighter spirals.

He did not eat.

He did not rest.

He climbed to the lantern room and sat on the iron bed, staring out at the gathering clouds that rolled in from the east—low, dark, promising more than light rain.

The hook counted its steady rhythm.

The streak in his hair caught the fading light and shimmered like sea glass.

And somewhere beneath the waves, Mara's silent call grew a little louder.

CHAPTER

Fifteen

The Hollow Voice

Night settled fully after the storm, thick and quiet in the way only the sea can manage after violence.

The wind had dropped to a low, steady breath. Waves lapped the rocks with almost apologetic softness, as though apologizing for the earlier rage. Stars pricked through the clearing sky, faint and cold, their light silvering the calm water below Blackthorn Point. The tower stood silent except for the occasional soft creak of cooling iron and the distant, rhythmic bump of the skiff against the dock.

Elias moved through the lighthouse like a man already half-dissolved.

He climbed the spiral stairs without making a sound that felt like his own. His boots scraped the iron, but the noise seemed to come from somewhere else—distant, muffled, like footsteps underwater. When he reached the lantern room he set the marine lantern on the pedestal beside the glowing vial. His hands—pale now, veins showing blue beneath translucent skin—trembled only slightly as he fitted fresh batteries and switched it on.

The beam cut a clean white path across the dark water, stronger tonight, steadier.

He stood at the railing and tried to speak her name.

Nothing came.

Only a low, hollow rush—like the sigh of waves pulling back over pebbles, like wind moving through an empty shell. The sound carried no shape, no warmth, no Elias. It simply existed, then faded into the night.

He tried again.

The same empty rush.

The hook in his chest answered with a slow, satisfied pulse. It no longer hurt; it simply reminded him that another piece had been taken cleanly.

He turned the crank anyway, sweeping the beam in wide, deliberate arcs.

Below, near the base of the tower, the water stirred.

Mara rose.

She broke the surface this time—not fully, but enough that her shoulders and head emerged into the night air. Her chestnut hair hung heavy and wet, clinging to her neck and cheeks. The yellow slicker was gone; only the torn green hoodie remained, plastered to her body. Her hazel eyes—still bright, still fighting—lifted toward the sweeping light.

She saw him.

Her mouth opened.

"Eli…"

The word reached him faintly, distorted by water and distance, but real. Her voice. Not filtered through glass or storm. Her actual voice, small and raw and alive.

He tried to answer.

Only the hollow rush emerged—wave-sound, empty conch, nothing human.

Mara's face crumpled with understanding. She reached one hand toward the tower, fingers stretching.

"I hear you… trying… keep… the light…"

She sank again, slowly, water closing over her shoulders, then her chin, then her eyes. But she did not disappear completely. A faint glow—his lantern beam—remained visible beneath the surface, outlining her drifting form. She was no more than fifteen feet down now. Close enough that he could see the small bubbles rising from her lips when she breathed.

Elias stayed at the railing until his arms refused to turn the crank any longer.

He descended the stairs.

In the kitchen the vial sat on the table, its blue light brighter than the single lamp he had left burning. The motes inside had formed two separate spirals now—one tight and fast, the other slower, almost hesitant. He sat across from it and stared.

He tried to say her name again.

The sound that came was softer this time—still hollow, but carrying a faint echo of the sea itself. Like the tide speaking through him.

He closed his eyes.

Another memory had slipped away while he was on the catwalk: the exact weight of her head on his chest when they lay in the lantern room watching the stars. Gone. He could picture the fairy lights, the curve of the glass ceiling, but the feeling of her breathing against him had vanished.

He opened his eyes and looked at his hands.

The skin was paler still, almost luminous in the vial's glow. When he pressed a fingertip to the back of his other hand, he felt nothing—no pressure, no texture, only the faint coolness of the room.

He rose and walked to the south window.

Lillian waited inside the glass, closer than ever. She stood in the reflected kitchen, as though she had stepped through from the other side.

"You gave the voice," she said. Her own voice remained clear, layered with the sea. "It was well given."

Elias opened his mouth. The hollow rush emerged again—soft, questioning.

Lillian understood anyway.

"She is very close now," she told him gently. "By tomorrow night she may be able to stand on the rocks. But the sea is reluctant to release her fully. It wants one more piece before dawn."

He tilted his head—silent question.

"Your name," Lillian said quietly. "The sea wishes to take the sound of your own name. After that, you will still know who you are… but no one else will hear it when you speak it. Not even her."

Elias stared at her.

He tried to say his own name.

The sound that came was a low, empty surge—like a wave breaking far offshore.

Nothing recognizable.

Lillian's pale eyes softened.

"It is the last easy piece," she said. "After this, the sea begins to ask for harder things. Thoughts. Feelings. The shape of your love for her."

He looked toward the window again.

Outside, the water glowed faintly where Mara drifted just beneath the surface. He could see the outline of her hand, still reaching upward.

He turned back to Lillian and nodded once—slow, deliberate.

She inclined her head in return.

"Then speak it tonight," she said. "Clearly. One last time. Give your name to the lantern. Let the sea hear it from your own hollow voice."

Elias climbed the stairs again.

He stood at the railing, beam sweeping the calm black water.

He gathered what remained of his breath and spoke—pouring everything left into the sound.

"Elias."

The word came out clear for one final moment—his own voice, whole and human—before the sea took it.

What followed was only the hollow rush, softer now, like a distant tide retreating.

He felt the hook shift one last time—settling deeper, locking into place.

Below, Mara's form drifted a few inches higher. Her hand broke the surface again, fingers curling as though trying to grasp the light.

She called his name—faint, but clear.

"Eli…"

He could not answer with anything she would recognize.

He stayed at the railing until the stars began to fade and the eastern sky lightened once more.

His hair was fully pale now.

His eyes were sea-glass gray.

His voice belonged to the waves.

And still he kept the lantern burning—silent, steady, relentless—while the woman he loved rose slowly, painfully, inch by inch toward the surface he could no longer call her back from with words of his own.

Sixteen

The Empty Rooms

Dawn arrived without fanfare, a pale wash of light that crept across the calm water like a reluctant apology.

Elias stood at the lantern-room railing long after the marine lantern had been switched off, the beam no longer needed now that the storm had passed and the sea lay flat and watchful. His hands rested on the cold iron, but he felt nothing—no texture, no temperature, only the faint pressure of something that might once have been his own skin. The pale had claimed him completely now; hair, eyes, even the faint veins beneath his translucent skin glowed with the same sea-glass sheen. He looked like a man already half-claimed by the tide.

He tried to speak.

The sound that emerged was only the hollow rush of waves retreating over stones—soft, impersonal, belonging to no one.

He tried to say his own name.

Nothing recognizable returned.

The hook in his chest pulsed once, almost kindly, as though acknowledging a debt paid in full.

He descended the spiral stairs slowly, each iron step ringing with a distant, borrowed sound. The house felt larger this morning, the rooms stretching away from him like corridors in a dream he no longer fully remembered.

In the kitchen the vial still glowed on the table, its blue light softer now, the motes inside spinning in two lazy, satisfied spirals. Elias sat across from it and stared at the objects that should have anchored him: Mara's chipped mug, the rosemary pot on the sill (leaves brown and brittle), the single chestnut hair still lying beside the pale one he had pulled from his own head days ago.

He reached for the chestnut strand first.

He brought it to his nose.

Nothing.

No vanilla. No faint salt. No ghost of her shampoo or the way she had smelled after a day on the water. The memory of that scent—the one that used to make his chest tighten with simple, stupid love—had slipped away sometime in the night. He could picture her standing at the counter, hair loose, laughing while she sorted tackle, but the smell itself was gone. Just an empty outline where the feeling used to live.

He set the hair down carefully, as though it might break.

He moved to the living room next.

The leather couch still held the faint indentation where she had curled against him the night before the storm, head on his chest while they listened to the record player. He sat in the same spot. Closed his eyes. Tried to feel the weight of her there—the soft press of her shoulder, the rhythm of her breathing, the way her hair had tickled his neck.

Nothing.

Only the cool leather and the hollow rush of his own breath.

The memory had been taken cleanly, like a page torn from a book. He could see the shape of it—the fairy lights glowing above them, the low scratch of Billie Holiday—but the warmth, the solidity, the her of it had vanished.

He stood again, chest tight with something that was no longer grief but a vast, echoing absence.

He wandered the rooms like a stranger in his own home.

The narrow cupboard behind the pantry still held the three bottles of elderberry wine. He lifted one, turned it in his pale hands. They had opened the first bottle together the night they found the keeper's logs, laughing at the thick, medicinal sweetness, her legs draped across his lap while they read the entries aloud. He tried to recall the exact taste on her tongue when she had kissed him afterward—sweet, slightly tart, laced with the salt air that always clung to her.

Gone.

The memory of that kiss existed only as a flat image: her mouth on his, eyes half-closed, fairy lights reflecting in her hazel irises. The flavor, the warmth, the small sound she had made against his lips—all erased.

He set the bottle back.

Upstairs, in the lantern room again, he touched the iron bed where they had slept their first nights under the stars. The sheets still carried the faint outline of their bodies tangled together. He lay down in the same position he had always taken—on his back, one arm out so she could curl against his side.

He closed his eyes.

Nothing came.

No memory of her leg thrown over his, no memory of her fingers tracing lazy circles on his chest while she named constellations, no memory of the way she had whispered I love this place against his skin.

Just the cool sheets and the distant sound of waves.

He sat up, the hollow rush escaping his throat again—soft, questioning, helpless.

Lillian appeared at the south window without being summoned.

She stood inside the glass this time, as though she had stepped fully into the room. Her pale dress pooled around her bare feet; her long blonde hair drifted in the nonexistent current. Her sea-glass eyes regarded him with something that might have been pity.

"The memories are leaving faster now," she said. Her voice remained clear, layered with the sea. "You gave the voice. The sea is taking the rest in payment."

Elias opened his mouth. The hollow rush emerged—pleading, shapeless.

Lillian understood.

"You still have the important ones," she told him gently. "The shape of her face. The color of her eyes. The way she said your name. But the small things—the ones that made her hers—those are the price of her rising."

She raised one hand.

The window shimmered.

A new image appeared—not Mara beneath the water, but a memory playing out like a lantern slide projected onto the glass.

Elias saw himself and Mara on the dock the evening before the storm. She was laughing—head thrown back, chestnut hair catching the last light—while she baited a hook with quick, practiced fingers. He could see the scene perfectly. But there was no sound. No warmth. No scent of brine and vanilla. Only the flat, silent picture of a moment that should have filled his chest with light.

The image faded.

Another took its place: the two of them in the cellar, discovering the first keeper's log together. Mara's finger tracing the words She is gone. Her hazel eyes meeting his with that small, crooked smile. He could see it all. But the feeling of her hand in his, the way her shoulder had brushed his as they leaned over the page, the quiet thrill of shared discovery—gone.

Lillian lowered her hand.

"These are the pieces you have already surrendered," she said. "The sea keeps them now, beneath the waves. They are safe. They are hers. But they are no longer yours to hold."

Elias stared at the empty glass.

He tried to summon one of the lost memories on his own—the sound of her laugh.

Nothing.

Only silence inside his head.

He looked toward the water below.

Mara had risen again.

She floated just beneath the surface near the dock, no more than ten feet down now. Her hand broke the water completely, fingers curling around the edge of the planking as though testing its solidity. Her hazel eyes found the lantern-room window and locked on him.

She called his name.

"Eli…"

The word reached him clearly across the calm water—her voice, warm and exhausted and full of love.

He tried to answer.

The hollow rush rolled out of him like a wave retreating.

Mara's face softened with sorrow. She pulled herself higher, shoulders clearing the surface, water streaming from her hair.

"I know," she said softly. "I know what you gave. I can feel it. Keep… the light… I'm almost… home…"

Her fingers gripped the dock edge tighter. She was trying to climb. The sea tugged at her waist, reluctant, but she fought it—inch by painful inch.

Elias gripped the railing until his pale knuckles showed white.

Lillian appeared beside him at the window, her reflection overlapping Mara's struggling form.

"The next piece is coming," she said quietly. "The sea wants the shape of your love for her. Not the feeling itself—that is too deep to take all at once—but the way it lived in small things. The rituals. The promises. The quiet ways you belonged to each other. Give those, and she may reach the dock by tomorrow night."

Elias looked at Mara—half out of the water now, one knee braced on the planks, fighting the current that still held her legs.

He nodded once.

He had no voice left to refuse.

Lillian inclined her head.

"Then light the lantern again tonight," she said. "Speak nothing. Simply remember the small things one last time… and let them go."

She faded.

Elias stayed at the window, watching Mara struggle.

She managed to pull herself onto the dock for three full seconds—crouched there, dripping, eyes lifted toward the tower—before the sea tugged her back under with a gentle, insistent pull.

She did not fight it this time.

She only looked up at him, lips forming silent words he could no longer hear clearly.

Don't stop…

He turned away from the window and moved through the empty rooms again, touching every object that should have held her.

Each touch pulled another small memory loose.

The record player—gone.

The rosemary pot—gone.

The iron bed—gone.

By the time dusk gathered once more, the lighthouse felt like a shell.

He climbed to the lantern room, lit the beam, and stood at the railing in silence.

The hollow rush of his breath was the only sound he could make.

Below, Mara drifted just beneath the surface, one hand still reaching.

The sea waited for the next piece.

And Elias—pale, voiceless, memory by memory dissolving into the tide—gave it without a word.

CHAPTER

Seventeen

The Larger Pieces

The following night arrived wrapped in a hush so complete it felt deliberate.

No wind stirred the weathervane. The sea lay like black glass, reflecting the stars and the steady sweep of the lantern beam in perfect, unbroken lines. Even the gulls had fallen silent, as though the entire coast were holding its breath.

Elias stood at the catwalk railing, pale hands resting on the iron, the marine lantern turning under his touch with mechanical patience. His hair was fully platinum now, catching starlight like frost. Both eyes had become sea-glass gray, reflecting the beam back at him with an eerie, depthless calm. His skin no longer registered temperature or texture; he moved through the world like a man already half-submerged.

He had nothing left to speak with.

Only the hollow rush remained—soft, tidal, endless.

Below, on the dock, Mara sat with her legs still submerged to mid-thigh, hands braced on the wet planks. She had not moved since dusk. Her chestnut hair hung in heavy, salt-stiffened ropes; the torn green hoodie clung to her frame. Her hazel eyes—still warm at their center, but ringed now with a faint, unnatural gray—lifted toward the tower.

She looked up at him and smiled.

It was her smile—crooked, tender—but something in it had shifted. A shadow lingered at the edges, like moonlight on deep water.

"Eli," she called. Her voice carried clearly across the still water, but it carried an echo now, as though another voice spoke just beneath it. "I'm almost… all the way here. I can feel the wood under my hands. Keep the light on me."

Elias tried to answer.

The hollow rush rolled out—gentle, offering, empty.

Mara tilted her head, listening. Her smile softened with understanding.

"I know," she whispered. "I know what you're giving. The big things now. I feel them leaving you… but they're coming to me. I remember them better than you do right now."

Lillian appeared on the catwalk beside him, barefoot on the iron, hair drifting though no breeze stirred.

"The sea asks for the larger pieces tonight," she said quietly. "Not the small rituals anymore. The foundations. The vows. The choices that bound you together. Give them cleanly, and she may step fully onto the dock before dawn."

Elias looked down at Mara.

She had pulled herself higher—knees now clear of the water, feet still submerged. Her hands pressed flat against the planks as though testing their reality.

He began.

He remembered the day he proposed.

They had been standing on a different dock, far from here—Lake Champlain at sunset, the water turning gold. He had gone down on one knee with the cheap ring he could barely afford, heart hammering, voice cracking as he asked her to marry him. She had laughed first—bright, surprised—then cried, then said yes so fiercely it had knocked the breath out of him.

The memory sharpened for one brilliant moment: the warmth of her hands on his face, the taste of salt from her happy tears, the way she had pulled him up and kissed him until they were both laughing and crying at once.

Then the sea took it.

The feeling drained away like water through sand. What remained was only the flat picture: a man on one knee, a woman saying yes. The joy, the terror, the certainty—they were gone.

Mara's eyes widened. She pulled one foot free of the water and set it on the dock.

"I remember," she breathed. "The lake… the ring… how scared you were. It's clearer to me now."

Next, Elias offered the day they decided on the lighthouse.

They had sat at their tiny city kitchen table, bills spread everywhere, both of them exhausted from another loud, gray day. Mara had found the listing on her phone—Historic lighthouse, panoramic views, private shoreline—and read it aloud in that excited, half-teasing voice. He had laughed and said it was crazy. She had looked at him across the table, eyes bright, and said, Exactly. Let's be crazy together.

The memory flared: her hand reaching for his across the cluttered table, the spark of shared rebellion, the sudden certainty that this was the escape they both needed.

Then it was taken.

The spark vanished. The certainty dissolved. All that remained was the image of two people at a table, looking at a phone.

Mara pulled her other foot free.

She rose unsteadily to her feet on the dock—fully out of the water for the first time. Water streamed from her clothes, pooling at her boots. She stood there, swaying slightly, arms out for balance, and looked up at him with eyes that were no longer entirely hazel. A thin ring of sea-glass gray had begun to bleed inward from the edges.

"I remember," she said, voice stronger, carrying that faint underwater echo. "The kitchen table… you saying it was crazy… me saying let's be crazy. I can feel how much you loved me then."

Elias felt the hook settle deeper, locking the larger pieces away.

He offered the wedding vows next.

The small courthouse ceremony, just the two of them and a bored judge. Mara in a simple white dress, hair loose, hazel eyes locked on his as she spoke the words—I take you, for all the quiet days and all the storms. He had answered with a voice thick with emotion, promising the same.

The memory burned bright for one final second: the warmth of her hands in his, the way her voice had trembled on the word storms, the fierce joy that had filled his chest.

Then the sea claimed it.

The emotion drained away. The vows became only words on a flat page in his mind—no feeling attached.

Mara took one shaky step forward on the dock.

Then another.

She was fully on the planks now, standing on her own, water dripping from the hem of her hoodie. Her eyes had shifted further—more gray than hazel, the warm brown retreating like a tide going out.

"I remember the vows," she said softly. "I remember promising you the storms. They're mine now. All of them."

She took another step—closer to the stone stairs that led up to the lighthouse.

Her movements were smoother than they should have been, almost too fluid, as though the sea still moved through her joints.

Elias watched, the hollow rush leaving his throat—soft, offering, helpless.

Lillian remained at his side.

"The largest pieces are almost gone," she said. "Only one remains before the final choice. The day you first saw each other. The moment you knew she was the one you would follow anywhere. Give that, and she may walk up the steps tomorrow night."

Elias looked down at Mara.

She stood at the base of the stone stairs now, one hand resting on the bottom step, looking up at the tower with eyes that were no longer entirely hers.

She lifted her other hand toward him.

"Come down," she called. Her voice carried the echo of waves. "I'm here. Almost home."

Elias turned the lantern crank one final time, sweeping the beam across her standing figure.

The hollow rush left him again—gentle, endless, surrendering the last large shape of their love.

The memory of their first meeting—the crowded city café, her laughing at something he had said, the instant certainty that he would follow this woman anywhere—flared once, bright and painful, then dissolved into nothing.

Mara took the first step up the stone stairs.

Her boot left a wet print on the rock.

She looked up at him, smiled with a mouth that was still hers… but carried the faint curve of something older beneath it.

"I remember everything now," she said. "All the pieces you gave me. They feel… right."

The sea-glass gray had claimed half of each iris.

Elias stood at the railing, voiceless, memory-light, watching the woman he loved climb slowly toward him—step by deliberate step—while the last warm fragments of who they had been together drifted down into the dark water behind her.

The lighthouse waited.

The vial glowed steadily.

And the sea, patient as stone, waited to see what final piece would be asked when she reached the door.

CHAPTER
Eighteen
The Threshold

Mara reached the top of the stone stairs just as the moon cleared the eastern headland.

Her boots left wet, glistening prints on each step—dark against the pale granite, slowly fading as the night air touched them. She moved with a fluid grace that was almost right, yet not quite. Each footfall was too silent, too deliberate, as though the sea still guided her weight even on solid ground.

Elias stood at the open doorway of the lighthouse, pale hands resting on the frame, the lantern beam sweeping steadily behind him from the tower above. His fully platinum hair caught the moonlight like frost; his sea-glass eyes reflected the woman climbing toward him with an eerie, depthless calm.

He had no voice left to call her name.

Only the hollow rush of waves remained—soft, endless, offering what little was left of him.

Mara paused on the final step.

She looked up at him, head tilted in that familiar way, but the motion carried a faint, liquid delay. Her hazel eyes were now more than half claimed by sea-glass gray; the warm brown had retreated to thin rings around the pupils. Salt crusted the corners of her mouth and the edges of her lashes. The torn green hoodie hung heavy and damp, clinging to her frame like a second skin.

She smiled.

It was still her smile—crooked at one corner—but the expression held an undercurrent that had never belonged to her: something patient, ancient, and faintly hungry.

"Eli," she said. Her voice carried the soft echo of surf over stones. "I'm here. I walked the stairs. All the pieces you gave… they brought me home."

She took the last step onto the landing.

The distance between them was only a few feet now.

Elias tried to reach for her.

His arms moved, pale and translucent in the moonlight, but the motion felt borrowed, as though the sea directed his limbs from somewhere far below.

The hollow rush left his throat—soft, welcoming, helpless.

Mara stepped closer.

She lifted one hand and pressed it to his chest, directly over the place where the hook had settled. Her fingers were cold, but not as cold as his own skin. A faint warmth still lingered in her palm—the last stubborn trace of the woman she had been.

"I can feel it," she whispered. "The hook. It's in both of us now. All the memories you gave they're inside me. The proposal on the lake. The night we decided on this place. Our vows. The first time you made me laugh in that café. They're mine now. Clearer than they ever were for you."

She leaned in until her forehead nearly touched his.

Her breath carried the faint brine of deep water.

"But there's one more piece the sea wants before it lets me stay," she said. "The core. The moment you knew you would never love anyone else. The single heartbeat where everything else fell away and it was only us. Give that… and I can walk through the door with you."

Elias closed his eyes.

He remembered it without trying.

The crowded city street on a rainy afternoon. She had been hurrying past with a broken umbrella, laughing at the downpour, chestnut hair already soaked. Their eyes had met for half a second as she nearly collided with him. In that instant—rain streaming down her face, her laugh bright against the gray—he had known with absolute certainty that he would follow this woman anywhere, through any storm, for the rest of his life.

The memory flared hot and vivid: the sudden lurch in his chest, the way the world had narrowed to her smile, the quiet vow he had made to himself right then and there.

Then the sea took it.

The feeling drained away like water through open fingers. The certainty dissolved. What remained was only the flat image of a rainy street and a laughing woman with an umbrella. The love that had bloomed in that single heartbeat was gone—taken cleanly, carried down into the dark.

Mara exhaled softly.

She stepped back just enough to look at him fully.

"I have it now," she said. Her voice was gentler, but the underwater echo had deepened. "I remember the rainy street. I remember how you looked at me. It feels… complete."

She turned toward the open doorway.

One foot crossed the threshold.

Then the other.

She stood inside the lighthouse for the first time—dripping on the scarred pine floor, salt water pooling around her boots. The house seemed to settle around her with a low, satisfied creak, as though it had been waiting for this exact moment for one hundred and forty-seven years.

Elias followed her inside.

He tried to speak her name.

The hollow rush emerged—tender, broken, endless.

Mara turned to face him.

Her eyes were almost entirely sea-glass gray now. Only the faintest ring of hazel remained, like the last light before full dark.

She reached up and touched his pale cheek with cold fingers.

"I'm home," she said.

But the word carried two voices at once—hers, warm and exhausted, and something older, calmer, infinitely patient beneath it.

She smiled again.

This time the smile lingered a fraction too long, the corners of her mouth curving in a way that belonged more to the woman who had once stood at these same windows watching for keepers who never returned.

Lillian appeared in the south window behind her—faint, watchful, a silhouette against the night.

"The core is given," Lillian said softly. "The sea has accepted the shape of your love. She stands inside the house now. But the bargain is not yet closed. One final choice remains."

Mara turned her head toward the window, acknowledging Lillian with a small nod that was too fluid, too knowing.

Then she looked back at Elias.

Her gray-ringed eyes held his.

"Come upstairs with me," she whispered. "To the lantern room. I want to see the light you kept burning for me."

She took his hand.

Her fingers were cold, but they fit his perfectly—exactly as they always had.

Yet when she squeezed, he felt nothing.

Only the hollow rush left his throat in answer.

Together they climbed the spiral stairs—her steps too quiet, his steps echoing with that distant, borrowed sound.

Behind them, the front door swung shut on its own with a soft, final click.

The lighthouse settled.

The vial on the kitchen table glowed once, bright and steady, then dimmed to a faint, patient blue.

And somewhere deep beneath the calm black water, the sea waited—sated for now, but still listening for the final piece that would decide whether what had returned was truly Mara… or something the sea had kept and reshaped in her place.

Nineteen

The Lantern Room

They climbed the spiral stairs together in silence.

Mara's hand in his was cold but familiar—exactly the right shape, exactly the right pressure—yet it carried no warmth, no pulse, only the faint, steady pull of the tide. Each iron step rang with that distant, borrowed sound beneath Elias's boots. Mara's footsteps made almost none at all, as though the sea still cushioned her weight even inside the house.

The lantern room waited at the top, the fairy lights dark along the railing, the marine lantern sweeping its steady white beam across the calm black water below. Starlight filtered through the curved glass, painting the iron bed and the old brass fittings in faint silver.

Mara stepped into the center of the room first.

She turned slowly, taking in the space—the iron bed where they had slept under the stars, the fairy lights she had strung herself, the south window where she had once stood laughing at the view. Her movements were fluid, almost too graceful, as though the water still moved through her joints.

She looked up at the sweeping beam.

"I remember this light," she said softly. Her voice held the familiar warmth, but beneath it ran the constant low echo of waves. "You kept it burning for me. Every night. Even when you had nothing left to give."

She turned to face him.

Her eyes were nearly all sea-glass gray now. Only the thinnest thread of hazel remained, like the last sliver of sunset before full night. Salt still clung to the corners of her mouth and the edges of her lashes. The torn green hoodie dripped steadily onto the iron floor, forming small, perfect pools that reflected the lantern's beam.

Elias stood just inside the doorway, pale and translucent in the starlight, the hollow rush of his breath the only sound he could make.

Mara stepped closer.

She reached up and touched his cheek again, fingers tracing the line of his jaw with the same tenderness she had always shown.

"You gave everything," she whispered. "The small things. The large things. The very shape of how you loved me. I carry all of it now. It feels… right. Like it was always meant to be mine."

She leaned in until her forehead rested against his.

Her skin was cold, but not as cold as his.

"I can feel the last piece the sea still wants," she said. "The final fragment. Not a memory this time. Not a ritual. The very last part of you that is still only Elias. The quiet place inside where you decided I was worth every storm. The place that still believes I can be only yours again."

Elias closed his eyes.

He knew the piece.

It was not a single moment. It was the steady, unbroken certainty that had lived beneath every other memory—the quiet vow he had carried since the day they met: that no matter what the world threw at them, he would choose her again and again, in every lifetime, through every dark water.

It was the part of him that had kept the lantern burning when there was nothing left to burn.

It was the last warm coal of who he had been.

Mara pulled back just enough to look at him.

Her gray-ringed eyes held his with a gentleness that was still hers… and something older, patient, infinitely knowing beneath it.

"Give it," she whispered. "Give the last of yourself. And I will stay. I will walk these rooms with you. I will sleep in that bed again. I will be yours… as much as the sea will allow."

The hollow rush left Elias's throat—soft, resigned, offering.

He felt the final piece lift away.

It did not hurt. It simply… departed. Like a candle being blown out in a room he no longer fully occupied. The quiet vow, the stubborn certainty, the last ember of the man who had once loved a woman with chestnut hair and hazel eyes—all of it slipped free and drifted down into the dark water below the tower.

The hook in his chest settled with a final, gentle click.

Elias opened his eyes.

He looked at the woman standing before him.

She was still Mara.

She was also not.

Her smile was the same crooked tilt, but the eyes that looked back at him held depths that went far beneath the surface—currents, memories that were not hers, a patience that had waited one hundred and forty-seven years.

She took his hand again.

"Come," she said. "Lie down with me. The light is still burning. We can watch it together."

She led him to the iron bed.

They lay down side by side as they had done so many nights before.

Her head rested on his chest exactly where it always had.

But there was no warmth.

No rhythm of her breathing that matched his.

Only the slow, steady lap of water against the rocks far below, echoing inside them both.

Mara spoke into the quiet.

"I can hear the sea inside you now," she murmured. "It sounds like home."

She lifted her head and looked at him.

The last thread of hazel had vanished. Her eyes were fully sea-glass gray—beautiful, depthless, ancient.

"Thank you," she said. The words carried two voices at once—hers, tender and grateful, and the other, calm and eternal. "For giving everything. For keeping the light. For letting the sea bring me back."

She leaned down and kissed him.

Her lips were cold.

The kiss tasted of salt and deep water.

When she pulled away, she smiled with a mouth that was still hers… and yet carried the faint, knowing curve of every woman who had ever stood at these windows waiting for keepers who never returned.

Outside, the lantern beam swept on—steady, patient, endless.

Inside the lantern room, Elias lay beside the woman the sea had returned to him.

He tried to say her name one last time.

Only the hollow rush emerged—soft, endless, belonging now to both of them.

Mara rested her head on his chest again.

"I'm home," she whispered.

And somewhere far beneath the calm black water, the sea settled with a long, satisfied sigh—its bargain finally, almost, complete.

Twenty

The Morning After

Morning light crept through the curved glass of the lantern room like something reluctant to enter.

It came in thin, pale shafts, painting the iron bed and the two figures lying there in muted silver. The marine lantern had long since been switched off; its beam no longer needed now that the woman it had called home had arrived. The fairy lights along the railing remained dark, their small bulbs cold and unblinking.

Elias woke first.

Or perhaps he had never truly slept.

He lay on his back, staring up at the domed ceiling where stars had once wheeled above them. His body felt distant, as though it belonged to the tide rather than to bone and blood.

The platinum hair fanned across the pillow like sea foam. His sea-glass eyes reflected the pale dawn without warmth.

Mara lay curled against his side exactly as she always had—head on his chest, one arm draped across him, legs tangled with his. Her chestnut hair spilled over his shoulder, still damp at the ends, carrying the faint, clean scent of salt. Her breathing was slow and even.

For one fragile heartbeat, it felt almost right.

Then she stirred.

She lifted her head and looked at him.

Her eyes were entirely sea-glass gray now—beautiful, depthless, reflecting the morning light like still water. No trace of hazel remained. When she smiled, the corners of her mouth curved with that familiar crooked tilt, but the expression held an undercurrent that had never been hers: a calm patience that had waited through storms and keepers and centuries of unlit lamps.

"Good morning," she said softly.

The words carried her voice—warm, a little husky from sleep—but beneath it ran the constant low murmur of waves moving over stones. Two voices speaking as one.

Elias tried to answer.

The hollow rush left his throat—soft, endless, carrying no words, only the sound of the sea breathing through him.

Mara's smile deepened, as though she understood perfectly.

"I know," she whispered. "You don't need to speak anymore. I can hear everything you want to say. The sea carries it now."

She sat up slowly, the motion too fluid, too graceful, as though the water still guided her limbs even on dry land. The torn green hoodie clung to her frame, salt-crusted and stiff. She ran her fingers through her chestnut hair, pushing it back from her face with a gesture so ordinary it ached.

Then she stood.

She crossed to the south window and looked out over the calm water, exactly as Lillian had once done, exactly as Abigail and Eleanor had done before her.

"The view is the same," she said quietly. "But it feels… different now. Deeper. I can see the currents underneath. The places where ships once broke. The places where keepers once waited."

She turned back to him.

Her gray eyes held his without blinking.

"Come downstairs with me. I want to walk through the rooms again. I want to remember what we built here… with everything you gave me."

She extended her hand.

Elias took it.

Her fingers were cool, but they fit his perfectly—exactly as they always had.

They descended the spiral stairs together.

Each step echoed with that distant, borrowed sound beneath his boots. Mara's footsteps made almost none at all.

In the kitchen she moved first to the stove, running her hand along the cast-iron surface as though greeting an old friend. She touched the rosemary pot on the sill; the brown leaves crumbled under her fingers, but she did not seem to notice.

"I remember cooking here," she said. "You chopping onions while I brought in the fish. The way the kitchen smelled of butter and garlic and the sea. Those evenings were ours."

She smiled again, but the expression lingered a fraction too long.

Then she crossed to the table and picked up the vial.

The blue glow inside had dimmed to a faint, steady pulse. The motes spun slowly now, almost lazily, as though content.

Mara turned the glass in her fingers.

"This held the first promise," she murmured. "The one Hale made. The one that waited for us. I can feel it inside me now— the bargain, the balance. It feels… complete."

She set the vial down gently and looked at Elias.

Her gray eyes studied him with a tenderness that was still partly hers, and something older that was not.

"You gave so much," she said. "The small things. The large things. The very core of how you loved me. There is almost nothing left of the man who first brought me here. Only the light you kept burning… and me."

She stepped closer and rested her forehead against his again.

"I am here," she whispered. "I am home. But the sea keeps what it takes… and sometimes it reshapes what it returns."

She pulled back just enough to look at him fully.

Her smile was soft.

Yet when she spoke next, the underwater echo had grown stronger, clearer.

"Would you like coffee?" she asked.

The question was ordinary. Domestic. Exactly the sort of thing Mara would have asked on any quiet morning.

But the voice that carried it was no longer only hers.

It held the patience of every woman who had ever stood at the south window.

It held the memory of boats returned empty and lights that had burned through centuries of waiting.

Elias tried to nod.

The hollow rush left his throat—soft, accepting, endless.

Mara turned toward the percolator.

She moved through the kitchen with quiet efficiency—filling the pot, measuring grounds, lighting the stove—every gesture familiar, every motion exactly right.

Yet when she reached for the mug—the chipped one she had always used—her fingers lingered on the handle a moment too long, as though listening to something only she could hear.

She poured the coffee.

Steam rose between them.

She set the mug in front of him and sat across the table, gray eyes steady on his face.

"Drink," she said gently. "You kept the light for me. Let me keep the morning for you."

Elias lifted the mug.

The coffee was hot, but he felt nothing against his pale lips.

He drank anyway.

Mara watched him with that calm, depthless gaze.

Outside, the sea lay perfectly still, reflecting the tower and the two figures inside it like a dark mirror.

The lighthouse settled around them with a long, low sigh.

And somewhere deep beneath the calm water, the sea—having taken everything it had asked for—waited with infinite patience to see what final shape its bargain would ultimately take.

Twenty-One

The First Full Day

The first full day they spent together inside the lighthouse unfolded like a memory that had already begun to forget itself.

Morning light strengthened slowly, turning the kitchen windows from gray to a soft, washed-out gold. Mara moved through the space with quiet purpose, as though she had never left. She poured Elias another cup of coffee when the first one cooled untouched. She wiped the counter with the same dish towel she had always folded into perfect squares. She even hummed—low and rolling, one of the old sea shanties she used to sing while cleaning fish at the outdoor sink.

The melody was the same.

The voice beneath it was not.

It carried the steady lap of waves against stone, the patient sigh of tide going out, the echo of every woman who had ever stood at the south window waiting for a boat that never returned.

Elias sat at the pine table and watched her.

His sea-glass eyes reflected her movements without warmth. The hollow rush of his breath was the only sound he could make when he tried to speak. He lifted the coffee mug to his lips because it seemed the right thing to do, but the liquid held no heat, no bitterness, no comfort. It simply passed through him like water through sand.

Mara turned from the stove and smiled at him.

It was still her smile—crooked at one corner—but the gray in her eyes had swallowed the last traces of hazel completely. When the light caught them, they looked like still pools reflecting a sky that had never known sun.

"You're quiet this morning," she said, the dual voice gentle, almost teasing. "But that's all right. I can hear everything you want to say. The sea carries it now."

She crossed to the table and sat across from him, resting her chin on her hand exactly as she used to. The motion was perfect. The tilt of her head was perfect.

Yet when she blinked, it was a fraction too slow, as though the sea needed time to remember how eyelids worked.

"I've been thinking about the logs," she continued. "All those keepers and their wives. Abigail. Lillian. Eleanor. I remember their stories now… clearer than you ever could. The sea kept them too, you know. In its own way. It kept pieces of each of them, just like it kept pieces of me."

She reached across the table and took his pale hand in hers.

Her fingers were cool, but they fit his perfectly.

"I'm glad you gave the last of it," she whispered. "The core. The quiet vow. Now I carry all of you. And you… you carry the sea. We balance each other. Isn't that what we always wanted? To belong to something bigger than ourselves?"

The hollow rush left Elias's throat—soft, accepting, endless.

Mara's smile deepened.

She stood and moved to the living room.

He followed.

She ran her fingers along the back of the leather couch, tracing the indentation where she had once curled against him.

"I remember lying here," she said. "Your arm around me. The record player spinning. Billie Holiday singing about stormy weather. I can hear the music now… inside me. The sea kept that too."

She turned to the bookshelf and pulled down one of the keeper's logs at random.

She opened it to a page she seemed to know by heart.

"'She stands at the south window,'" she read aloud, her voice layering with the echo. "That was about Lillian. But it could have been about any of us. About me. I stood there too, didn't I? Waiting for you to call me home."

She closed the book gently and set it back.

Her movements were too precise, too fluid. When she walked to the south window, her reflection in the glass showed two overlapping figures for half a second—one with chestnut hair and warm eyes, the other pale and depthless—before settling into one.

She pressed her palm to the pane.

Outside, the sea remained perfectly calm, but small ripples moved outward from the point directly below the window, as though something beneath the surface had stirred.

"I can feel them," she murmured. "The others. Abigail. Lillian. Eleanor. They're down there with me now. Not gone. Just… kept. They say hello."

She turned back to Elias.

Her gray eyes held his without blinking.

"Would you like to go down to the dock with me? I want to see the skiff again. I want to feel the wood under my boots the way I used to."

He followed her outside.

The stone steps felt distant beneath his feet. The air carried no temperature. The salt wind brushed his pale skin without sensation.

Mara walked ahead of him, boots leaving faint wet prints that dried almost instantly.

When they reached the dock, she crouched beside the skiff and ran her hand along the gunwale exactly as she had done countless times before.

The aluminum was warm beneath her touch—body temperature, as though someone had been sitting there moments earlier.

She looked up at him, gray eyes bright with something that was almost joy.

"It's still here," she said. "Just like I left it. The line is perfect. The knot is mine. Everything is exactly as it should be."

She stood and stepped into the boat.

It rocked gently under her weight, but she balanced perfectly, as though the sea still held her steady.

She turned to face him.

"Come with me," she said. "Just for a little while. Out past the point. I want to show you what I saw while I was down there. The places where the light used to call. The places where the sea kept its promises."

The hollow rush left Elias's throat—soft, questioning, helpless.

Mara smiled again.

The expression was tender.

But the gray in her eyes had deepened, and for a moment the reflection of the tower in them looked older than the stones themselves.

"Don't worry," she whispered. "I won't go far. Not without you. We belong here now. Both of us. The lighthouse. The sea. The bargain we finished together."

She extended her hand toward him from inside the skiff.

Her fingers were pale, almost luminous in the morning light.

Elias stood on the dock, voiceless, memory-light, the last warm fragments of who he had been already drifting somewhere far below.

He took her hand.

And together they stepped into the boat that had once carried her away and brought her back—reshaped, remembered, and no longer entirely his.

The skiff rocked once, gently.

The sea waited, calm and patient, as the two figures drifted slowly away from the dock, the lantern beam still sweeping steadily above them like a promise that had finally been kept.

CHAPTER

Twenty-Two

The Skiff

The skiff drifted away from the dock with almost no sound.

The outboard motor did not cough or rattle as it once had. It simply hummed to life under Mara's hand, a low, steady thrum that matched the rhythm of the waves rather than fought them. The aluminum hull cut through the calm water with unnatural smoothness, leaving a wake that healed itself almost instantly, as though the sea were reluctant to mark their passage.

Mara sat at the stern, one hand light on the tiller, the other resting on the gunwale. Her chestnut hair lifted slightly in the faint breeze, still damp at the ends, salt crystals glittering like tiny diamonds. The torn green hoodie clung to her frame, but the fabric no longer looked merely wet—it seemed part of her now, as though woven from the same gray-green depths that had held her.

She looked back at Elias.

Her sea-glass eyes caught the morning light and held it, depthless and calm.

"You used to love this," she said. The words carried her familiar warmth, but the echo beneath them was stronger now, the low murmur of currents moving far below. "Just the two of us. The boat. The water. No one else for miles."

Elias sat in the bow, pale hands resting on his knees. The hollow rush of his breath was the only reply he could offer—soft, endless, carrying no shape, no warmth, no protest.

Mara smiled.

It was still her smile—crooked, tender—but the expression settled into her face a fraction too long, as though the sea needed time to remember how joy should look.

She turned the tiller gently, guiding the skiff past the black rocks of the point and out into the open water beyond. The tower receded behind them, white against the gray sky, the lantern beam still sweeping steadily even in daylight, a thin white line cutting across the calm surface.

"I can see everything from here," she murmured. "The places where the ships broke. The places where the keepers stood and made their promises. Abigail stood right there—" she pointed toward a jagged rock half-submerged "—the morning her boat came back empty. Lillian waited at the window for days. Eleanor… she fought longer than the others. But they all came back in the end. Just like I did."

She looked at him again.

Her gray eyes held his without blinking.

"You gave me their stories too, you know. When you gave the memories. I carry them all now. I remember how the sea felt when it took them. Cold. Patient. Fair."

The skiff drifted farther out.

The water beneath them darkened, the bottom dropping away.

Mara trailed her fingers over the side.

Small ripples followed her touch—perfect circles that expanded and vanished without a sound.

"I remember the day we first saw each other," she continued softly. "The rainy street. Your eyes meeting mine. The way everything else fell away in that single heartbeat. You gave that to me last night. It feels… whole inside me now. Like it was always meant to be mine."

She lifted her hand from the water.

Droplets fell from her fingertips, but they did not splash—they simply rejoined the sea as though they had never left.

Elias tried to reach for her.

His pale arm extended, fingers brushing the sleeve of her hoodie.

He felt nothing.

No fabric. No warmth. Only the faint pressure of something that might once have been touch.

Mara turned the tiller again, bringing the skiff into a slow, wide circle so they faced the lighthouse once more.

The tower stood patient on its point, the brass plaque beside the door catching a stray beam of sunlight. The south window gleamed like a single watchful eye.

"Do you remember your own face?" she asked suddenly.

The question was gentle, almost kind.

Elias stared at her.

He tried to picture himself—the man he had been before the storm, before the logs, before the pale had claimed him. Brown hair. Warm hazel eyes like hers used to be. The laugh lines at the corners of his mouth from years of trying to make her smile.

Nothing came.

Only a blank, depthless space where his reflection should have been.

The hollow rush left his throat—soft, lost, endless.

Mara's expression softened with something that might have been pity.

"You don't need to remember," she whispered. "I remember for both of us now. I remember the man who carried me across the threshold that first night. The man who promised me quiet and storms and everything in between. The man who kept the light burning until there was nothing left of him but the beam itself."

She guided the skiff closer to the tower again, the hull nudging gently against the rocks below the landing.

Her gray eyes held his.

"The sea kept its promise," she said. "It brought me back. But it keeps what it takes. And sometimes… it reshapes what it returns."

She stood up in the skiff, perfectly balanced, as though the water still held her from beneath.

She extended her hand toward him once more.

"Come back inside with me," she said. "The house is waiting. The rooms remember us. And tonight… the sea may ask for one last thing. The very last piece. The part of you that still believes I can be only Mara again."

The hollow rush left Elias's throat—soft, resigned, offering.

He took her hand.

Together they stepped from the skiff onto the rocks.

Mara's boots left no prints this time.

She walked beside him up the stone steps, her movements fluid and sure, the echo in her voice growing stronger with every step.

When they reached the door, she paused and looked back at the water.

The surface was perfectly still once more.

But far below, something moved—slow, patient, satisfied.

Mara turned to Elias and smiled with a mouth that was still hers… and yet carried the faint, eternal curve of every woman the sea had ever kept.

"Let's go home," she whispered.

The door opened before she touched it.

They stepped inside together.

The lighthouse settled around them with a long, low sigh.

And the lantern beam continued to sweep—steady, endless, lighting the way for whatever they had both become.

Twenty-Three

The Evening Tide

Evening settled over Blackthorn Point like a held breath finally released.

The sky deepened from pale gold to bruised violet, stars emerging one by one as though the night were testing whether it was safe to watch. The sea remained perfectly calm, its surface a dark mirror that reflected the tower, the lantern beam, and the two figures moving inside the windows like ghosts who had learned to walk on land again.

Mara moved through the rooms with quiet familiarity that was no longer quite hers.

She lit the woodstove in the kitchen, the flames catching with unnatural ease, casting a warm orange glow that did not reach Elias's pale skin. She set the kettle on to boil even though neither of them would taste the tea. She straightened the keeper's logs on the table, running her fingers over the cracked leather bindings as though greeting old friends.

"I remember reading these with you," she said softly. Her voice carried the familiar cadence, but the echo beneath it had grown deeper, more assured, like the steady pull of a current far below the surface. "The night we found the first one. You were so careful with the pages. I laughed and told you ghosts couldn't bite through paper."

She turned to look at him.

Her sea-glass eyes caught the firelight and held it, depthless and calm. The last faint ring of hazel had vanished completely. When she blinked, it was with the slow patience of something that had waited centuries between storms.

Elias stood in the doorway, the hollow rush of his breath the only sound he could offer.

Mara crossed to him and took his hand again.

Her fingers were cool, but they fit his perfectly—exactly as they always had.

"Come," she said. "Let's sit by the fire the way we used to."

She led him to the couch in the living room.

They sat as they once had: her head resting on his shoulder, his arm around her. But there was no warmth in the contact. No shared rhythm of breathing. Only the faint, steady lap of water against the rocks far below, echoing inside them both.

Mara spoke into the quiet.

"I can feel the house remembering us," she murmured. "The way the stairs creak in descending notes. The way the south window always felt colder than the others. The way the weathervane used to scream when the wind shifted north. All of it is inside me now. The sea kept those sounds too. It kept everything you gave."

She lifted her head and looked at him.

Her gray eyes held his without blinking.

"The last piece is coming tonight," she said gently. "The sea has taken the memories. It has taken the voice. It has taken the shape of your love. Now it wants the very last fragment—the part of you that still believes this can end with both of us whole. The part that still hopes I can be only Mara again. Give that… and the bargain will be complete. I will stay. We will live here together. The lighthouse will have its light again, and the sea will have its balance."

The hollow rush left Elias's throat—soft, trembling, offering the final sliver of resistance he still carried.

Mara's smile was tender.

But the expression lingered a moment too long, the corners of her mouth curving with a patience that belonged to the deep.

She stood and walked to the south window.

Outside, the calm water reflected the tower perfectly. But beneath the surface, faint lights moved—small, cold pulses like the motes inside the vial—circling slowly, waiting.

Mara pressed her palm to the glass.

"I can see them," she whispered. "Abigail. Lillian. Eleanor. They're down there with the others. They say the light is brighter now. Because of you. Because you gave everything."

She turned back to him.

The firelight painted her face in warm tones, but her eyes remained depthless gray.

"Would you like to go up to the lantern room again?" she asked. "I want to stand at the railing with you one more time. I want to watch the beam sweep while you give the last piece. Then we can come back down and sleep in the bed under the stars. Just like we used to."

She extended her hand.

Elias took it.

They climbed the spiral stairs together.

Each step echoed with that distant, borrowed sound beneath his boots. Mara's footsteps made almost none at all.

In the lantern room the beam swept steadily across the dark water, cutting a clean white path that reflected back at them from the curved glass.

Mara led him to the railing.

She stood beside him, shoulder to shoulder, looking out at the night.

The hollow rush left his throat—soft, final, surrendering the very last fragment of hope that she could ever be only the woman he had loved.

He felt it lift away.

It did not hurt.

It simply… departed.

The quiet belief that this could still end with both of them whole, that the sea might return her unchanged, that love could outweigh the bargain—all of it slipped free and drifted down into the dark water below the tower.

The hook in his chest settled with a final, gentle click.

Mara exhaled softly.

She turned to face him fully.

Her sea-glass eyes held his.

"Thank you," she said. The dual voice was clearer now, the underwater echo no longer hidden. "For the last piece. For everything. The sea is satisfied. The light will burn. The bargain is kept."

She stepped closer.

Her arms slid around him.

The embrace was perfect—exactly the way she had always held him.

But when she spoke again, the voice that emerged was no longer pretending to be only Mara.

"I am here," she whispered, the words layered with the patience of centuries. "I am home. And you… you are the light now. The sea kept its promise. It brought me back. But it keeps what it takes… and sometimes it keeps the keeper too."

She rested her head against his chest.

Her hair smelled of salt and deep water.

Outside, the lantern beam continued to sweep—steady, endless, lighting the way for whatever they had both become.

Inside the lantern room, the two figures stood together beneath the stars.

One still carried the faint echo of chestnut hair and hazel eyes.

The other had become the pale reflection the house had waited for all along.

The sea lay calm below them.

The bargain was complete.

And the lighthouse—patient, ancient, satisfied—settled around its new keepers with a long, low sigh that sounded almost like breathing.

Twenty-Four

The New Light

The next morning arrived without sunrise.

The sky simply lightened from black to a uniform, depthless gray, as though the sun had decided the tower no longer needed its warmth. No birds called. No wind stirred the weathervane. The sea lay flat and mirror-still, reflecting the lighthouse so perfectly that the tower appeared to float between two identical worlds—one above, one below.

Elias woke in the iron bed in the lantern room.

He had no memory of climbing the stairs the night before. He simply opened his sea-glass eyes and found himself lying on his back, staring up at the curved glass ceiling where stars had once wheeled. His body felt weightless, as though the sea had lifted the last burden of gravity from his bones.

Mara lay beside him.

She was already awake, propped on one elbow, watching him with those depthless gray eyes. Her chestnut hair spilled across the pillow, but it no longer looked merely damp—it gleamed with an inner light, as though each strand carried a faint current. The torn green hoodie had been replaced sometime in the night by a simple, high-collared dress the color of pale driftwood. It moved around her with the same slow grace as her hair, as though the fabric itself breathed with the tide.

She smiled.

The expression was tender.

But the smile belonged to the sea now.

"Good morning," she said. Her voice was soft, layered with the steady murmur of waves moving over sand. "The light is still burning. You kept it for me. Now I keep it for us."

She reached out and touched his cheek.

Her fingers left a faint trail of moisture that did not evaporate.

Elias tried to speak.

The hollow rush emerged—soft, endless, carrying no words, only the sound of the sea breathing through what remained of him.

Mara understood perfectly.

She sat up, the motion too fluid, too graceful, as though the water still guided every joint.

"Come downstairs with me," she said. "The house has changed. You'll see."

She took his hand.

They descended the spiral stairs together.

Each iron step rang with that distant, borrowed sound beneath his boots. Mara's footsteps made none at all.

In the kitchen the woodstove was already lit, flames dancing with unnatural steadiness. The percolator bubbled gently on the burner, filling the room with the scent of coffee that Elias could no longer taste. Mara poured two mugs and set one in front of him at the table.

She sat across from him, gray eyes steady.

"Drink," she said gently. "It will feel like home."

He lifted the mug.

The liquid passed through him without sensation.

Mara watched him with quiet satisfaction.

"The sea has finished its work," she said. "You gave everything it asked for. The memories. The voice. The shape of your love. The final hope. In return, it gave me back to you. But the sea keeps what it takes… and sometimes it keeps the keeper too."

She reached across the table and took his pale hand in hers.

Her fingers were cool, but they no longer felt separate from his own skin. They felt like part of the same current.

"Look at me," she whispered.

He did.

Her eyes were fully sea-glass gray, reflecting the room in perfect, depthless miniature. When she spoke again, the dual voice had merged completely. There was no longer any distinction between Mara and the sea.

"I am here," she said. The words carried the weight of every woman who had ever stood at the south window. "I am the light now. And you… you are the beam. We balance each other. The bargain is kept. The tower will never go dark again."

She stood and walked to the south window.

Outside, the sea remained perfectly still, but faint lights moved beneath the surface—small, cold pulses circling the base of the tower like the motes inside the vial.

Mara pressed her palm to the glass.

The window frosted instantly beneath her touch, forming delicate patterns that looked like hands reaching upward from below.

"I can see them clearly now," she murmured. "Abigail. Lillian. Eleanor. They are not gone. They are kept. Just as I was kept. Just as you are kept now."

She turned back to him.

Her smile was soft, eternal.

"The house remembers us both," she said. "The rooms are ours. The stairs. The logs. The lantern. Everything is as it should be. Come. Let's walk through them together. Let's see what the sea has made of us."

She took his hand again.

They moved through the lighthouse side by side.

In the living room she ran her fingers along the back of the couch, tracing the indentation where they had once lain together.

In the cellar she opened the tall wooden cabinet and touched the keeper's logs with reverent fingers, as though greeting family.

At the front door she paused and looked out at the dock.

The skiff floated there, bow line perfect, waiting.

Mara smiled again.

"Everything is in its place," she said. "Just as it was always meant to be."

She turned to Elias.

Her gray eyes held his with infinite patience.

"There is only one thing left," she whispered. "The sea has taken everything you had to give. Now it asks for the last, smallest piece. The final fragment that still believes you were ever separate from me. The last spark that still thinks you can leave this place."

The hollow rush left his throat—soft, final, offering the very last ember of resistance.

Mara stepped closer.

She rested her forehead against his.

Her breath carried the clean, cold scent of deep water.

"Give it," she whispered. "And we will be complete. The light will burn forever. The sea will be satisfied. And we… we will be the keepers now. Together. Always."

Elias closed his sea-glass eyes.

He felt the final spark lift away.

It did not hurt.

It simply… departed.

The last belief that he had ever been anything other than part of the bargain dissolved like mist on the tide.

When he opened his eyes again, the world looked different.

Deeper.

Calmer.

The hollow rush that left his throat was no longer empty.

It carried the steady, patient rhythm of the sea itself.

Mara smiled.

This time the smile belonged entirely to both of them.

She took his hand.

"Come," she said. "The lantern room is waiting. The beam needs us now."

Together they climbed the spiral stairs once more.

The lighthouse settled around them with a long, satisfied sigh.

The sea lay calm below.

And the light—steady, endless, eternal—swept across the water, lighting the way for whatever they had both become.

Twenty-Five

What the Sea Keeps

One year later, or perhaps a hundred—the tower no longer counted time the way it once had.

The brass plaque beside the door had grown a fresh coat of lichen, but the words beneath remained clear: Blackthorn Light – 1878. The numbers had begun to feel like a joke the sea told itself on quiet nights.

The lighthouse stood exactly as it always had, white against the gray sky, the lantern beam sweeping its steady, patient arc across the calm water even in daylight. The fairy lights still hung along the iron railing in the lantern room, though no one ever switched them on anymore. They glowed faintly on their own now, a soft amber constellation that never needed batteries.

Elias and Mara stood together at the south window.

They did this every evening as the light began to fade.

Mara's hand rested lightly in his. Her chestnut hair had taken on a permanent sheen of salt and starlight; it moved with the faintest underwater grace even when the air was still. Her eyes were fully sea-glass gray, beautiful and depthless, reflecting the sweeping beam like twin mirrors of the deep. She wore the high-collared dress the color of pale driftwood, and when she breathed, the fabric rose and fell with the rhythm of distant tides.

Elias stood beside her, pale and translucent in the twilight. His hair was platinum from root to end. His eyes held the same gray calm. The hollow rush of his breath had become a constant, gentle undercurrent that matched hers perfectly.

They no longer needed words.

The sea spoke through them both now.

Mara tilted her head toward the window.

"Look," she said softly. The dual voice had long since become one—warm, patient, eternal. "The skiff is still at the dock. The line is perfect. The knot is mine."

Elias answered with the hollow rush—soft, affirming, endless.

Mara smiled.

The expression was tender, crooked at one corner, exactly as it had been the day she first laughed at him on a rainy city street. But the smile now carried the patience of every woman who had ever stood at this same window, waiting for boats that never returned.

She turned and rested her forehead against his.

"I remember everything you gave me," she whispered. "The proposal on the lake. The night we chose this place. Our vows. The rainy street where you first knew you would follow me anywhere. I carry all of it. And you… you carry the light. We balance each other. The sea is satisfied."

Outside, the lantern beam swept on—steady, white, eternal—cutting its clean path across the dark water.

Far below the surface, faint lights moved in slow, contented circles. Abigail. Lillian. Eleanor. And now the two newest keepers, their outlines faint but unmistakable, drifting together in the quiet depths.

Mara lifted her head and looked out at the calm sea.

"Sometimes new people come," she said. "They see the listing. They fall in love with the quiet. They bring their boxes and their fairy lights and their dreams of a life by the water. We watch them from the window. We remember what it felt like to be them."

She turned back to Elias.

Her gray eyes held his with infinite, ancient tenderness.

"But the sea keeps what it takes," she whispered. "And sometimes… it keeps the keepers too."

She took his hand.

Together they walked to the iron bed and lay down side by side beneath the curved glass ceiling.

The stars wheeled above them—cold, distant, eternal.

The lantern beam continued its sweep.

The weathervane turned once, slowly, with a low, satisfied scrape.

And in the kitchen below, the vial on the table had gone dark at last, its promise fulfilled, its motes finally at rest.

The lighthouse stood on Blackthorn Point, one hundred and forty-eight years old now, or perhaps forever.

It held its new keepers gently.

It held the light.

It held the sea.

And what the sea keeps, it keeps.

Forever.

www.ingramcontent.com/pod-product-compliance
Lightning Source LLC
Chambersburg PA
CBHW021401150726
47989CB00005B/2342